Mission: Murder

Ryker Bartley Mystery Book 1

A.M. Holloway

Your Book Company

Prologue

The moonless sky provides the perfect backdrop. Only one light burns in the house, and I know it's the desk lamp in the downstairs office. How do I know? Because I've been in this spot many times before, waiting.

At my set time, I enter the house through the back door, bypassing the security alarm. Stepping into the kitchen, I pause, letting my eyes adjust to the shadows. A kitchen island sits in the middle of the room, with many pots and pans hanging above. No one hears me. It's time.

My shoes make no noise on the hardwood floors as I creep through the kitchen and down the hallway to the office. I hear papers move. The desk chair rolls on its floor protector. Then a sigh. I stop. And listen. And wait.

Seconds fly by before I take my next step. Excitement courses through my veins as I creep closer to the office door. Sweat beads upon my brow and runs down my back. Deep breaths and the count of five help me slow my pulse and center myself. I peer around the office door to see the guy studying papers on his desk with the remains of his nightly drink sitting untouched in a tumbler under his desk lamp. Since he faces away from the door, I pounce.

The guy never had a chance. I slid a garrote around this guy's neck so fast, he never had time to get his fingers underneath. Within fourteen seconds, his face turned colors, then he slumped over, banging his head on the desk. I flinched. Did the lady hear the noise?

I left the unconscious guy sitting in his desk chair so I could finish my business. Footsteps on the stairs answered my earlier question. The lady heard the man's head hit the desk. With her almost to the office, I plastered my back to the wall next to the door. I was ready.

When the lady entered the room, she went straight for her husband. She screamed before I reached her. But the garrote made quick work of her neck, too. It didn't take fourteen seconds for her to droop in my arms. I left her propped against the desk on the floor. It made a pleasant scene.

My watch told me how much time I had spent inside. Two minutes to spare this time. Touching the necks of both victims, I felt for a pulse. Then I moved to their wrists. You never can be too sure. Nothing.

I left the house the same way I entered. The backyard was quiet as I passed the swimming pool. Then I slipped through a missing panel in their privacy fence behind the pool house. This neighborhood backed up to a park, convenient for me since I parked my truck there. However, some places I've been aren't this helpful.

After I climbed into my truck, I surveyed the area before pulling out my notebook. I couldn't take the chance of someone seeing my notes, although no one would understand them except me. This is a special notebook full of numbers which I keep in a safe place. I crossed through tonight's handiwork and looked forward to the next.

Chapter 1

Today, I pack the remnants of my last case into a cardboard box. I'm Ryker Bartley, Detective, with the Ft. Worth, Texas Police Department. I'm currently assigned to the violent crime division, but I help with other cases that have stumped my predecessors over the years.

My last cold case was from twenty years ago. Someone stabbed a young lady while she sat in her bathroom as she dressed for the day. Without leads, the case grew cold. Unfortunately, the victim's parents have both passed away, and there were no siblings. But that didn't mean we stopped looking for the killer.

I dug the box from the evidence room and got to work. A lot has changed with our technical advancements in DNA, blood spatter, and even photos in twenty years. Working with what I had, I read every interview twice, studied the pictures many times before one began forming in my mind.

If I've learned anything in my short stint as a detective, it's never to jump to conclusions. Evidence will solve the case if you follow it.

The victim was in her late twenties at the time of death, a college graduate, and worked at an ad agency downtown. She handled billing and had recently started learning how to write ads for major companies.

So why kill her?

Her off-and-on boyfriend had an alibi. I'd still like to talk with him again, so I added his name to the top of my list. The victim, Frieda, lived in a first-floor corner apartment. Back then, there were no parking lot cameras or those fancy doorbell videos. I was out of luck with that.

Thumbing through the box, I found notes around Frieda's work. The wording in these notes had me questioning Frieda's workmates. Was something happening at the ad agency that upset Frieda?

I photocopied the contact list from the case file so I could write on it. Then, after the boyfriend, I'd check with the ad agency. With my plan, I started making calls.

Several of her co-workers still worked at the ad agency, while others had moved on to the bigger, better ones. The more I spoke with her co-workers, the more I learned. While some people didn't remember Frieda, others knew exactly who she was. It turns out Frieda's manager wanted more than a working relationship. Frieda turned him down one Friday night. Instead, she went dancing with a group from work. Their relationship after that weekend was awkward. Frieda even considered finding a new job.

The detective describes their interrogation of the manager right after Frieda's death. He never confessed, but we never proved his alibi, either. Her manager moved to Austin within six months of her death.

Every crime scene photo lay on my desk. I studied each with a magnifying glass several times before leaning back in my chair, closing my eyes as I visualized the scene. What did we miss? I jumped to attention. That's it!

I lifted a photo from my desk, studying the bed. Someone touched the bed's corner. Maybe the killer tripped over the victim's shoes on the floor, and he used the bed to catch himself. Where are those bedsheets?

When I stuck my head in the box, I found the sheets folded in an evidence bag. I had the killer as long as the DNA remained, and he was in the system. After I delivered the sheets to the crime lab, I took myself to lunch. Anytime we handed over evidence from a cold case, we moved to the front of the line. My contact, Sheena, said I'd have the results in an hour or faster if the killer was in the system. She proved herself.

Sheena called, and we got him. The sheets had a bloody fingerprint that matched Frieda's manager. So there was no doubt who killed Frieda. Now, to find him. My commander, Greta Huxley, worked with Austin to capture Frieda's killer. That felt good.

Another case closed. The photos are always the last to go inside the box. One more glance, just one. You try to remember every victim, but as the cases come and go, that becomes impossible. Unless you're me.

"Hey, Sgt. Bartley, got a minute? I've got a good one for you." Officer Hutton leans into my office, grinning.

I slide a file to the side. "Bring it on, Officer Hutton. Lay it out for me." I smirk and sip coffee as I watch the show. Hutton opens his thick file and lays the crime scene photos in order, then he places a map at the bottom of the photo stacks. These guys always search for the one case I can't solve. So far, I'm winning, but there is always that one case, the one that stumps you and makes you crazy until you solve it.

"Here it is, Sgt. We have a burglary gang ransacking houses in the middle of the day. If someone is home, they cover the homeowner's face with a pillowcase without hurting them. They only steal electronics. We can't pinpoint where they will strike next." The frustration is fresh on Hutton's face.

"So you want me to solve your case for you, is that it, Officer Hutton?" I snickered because Officer

Hutton is a friend, and he knows I'll help anytime I can. I've proved that.

"Please solve it, Sgt. I'm tired of chasing this group. It's been months. Every time we conduct a stakeout, we miss them altogether, or they hit another street in our area but not close enough to capture. It's so frustrating," Hutton lets out a sigh but turns quiet when he sees me get to work.

I studied the photos, location of the victim's houses, and the surrounding area. Three minutes passed, and Officer Hutton thought he stumped me until I circled a spot on the map in red pen. "This is where the gang will strike tomorrow afternoon, and this area here is where they live."

Officer Hutton sat in his chair with his mouth hanging open. It fascinates Hutton to see me in action. "I've got to ask. How do you do that, Sgt.? We've studied this same information and never put it together."

"It's a long story. I'll tell you one day, Hutton" I watched him leave my office while studying his file, wondering how I do it, day in and day out.

After Hutton left my office, I leaned back in my worn-out desk chair and remembered the day as if it were yesterday. I enlisted in the army right out of high school. The army was my calling, or so I thought. With so much happening in the world, I wanted to make a difference. At 31 years old, I rode in a Humvee with my team. We rushed to help another team trapped in a gunfight. Our driver veered off the main road, striking an IED. The driver and the guy directly behind him perished in the accident. Three others survived with varying degrees of injuries. I survived after spending 44 days in a coma from a traumatic brain injury. Another guy lost a leg, while another guy lost an arm.

Our team picture taken two days before the accident sits upon my credenza. While I try not to dwell on the past, it still comes around whether I want it to.

When I awoke from the coma, the doctors labeled me an acquired savant. That was four years ago, almost to the day. So how am I supposed to tell others about my ability when I can't explain it, and it's in my head?

My day ended when I returned the cold case photos to their box, hopefully for good. Madge, my wife, called earlier to let me know she would work late again tonight. She's the head nurse in our downtown hospital's ER department. During our brief marriage, it seems one of us works late or at weird hours. For me, criminals never sleep, and for her, people get shot, have accidents, or get sick.

I walked outside into the late afternoon heat. Glancing at the sky, storms approached from the west. Those are the worst. They pack the most punch. As I reached my car, Jo, my partner, pulled her Crown Vic next to mine. "Hey, Bartley. Where are you going?"

"Home, I guess. I solved two today, so I thought I'd celebrate." I smiled. We've been partners since my career began here. She gets me, one of the few that does.

Jo shook her head, laughing, and replied, "you solved two cases today. And without me. How do you do it all by yourself?" We poke each other all day, every day. It keeps us going.

"Talent. That's all." I opened my car, then looked back at Jo. "What are you doing for supper? Want to grab a bite?" I asked, but I didn't know why. We've never been chummy outside of work, but today, I needed companionship. When the memories return, I turn solemn, and that's never good for me.

"Really? You're asking me out for supper. What gives, Bartley?" Jo's eyebrows bunched together because she knew something happened.

As I tried to play it safe, she pushed until I relented. I told her what happened with Officer Hutton. Once I explained, she traded her vehicle for mine because she knows the memories always get to me. We're comfortable together, and that's what happens when you spend more time with your work partner than you do with your life partner.

We dropped in on our favorite Mexican restaurant. Thankfully, we arrived before the nightly crowd. We enjoyed eating outside, but the weather prevented us from that pleasure. Then, halfway through the meal, the storm came. Thunder so loud you couldn't hear the other person's voice. Lucky for us, our server delivered our meal before the lights went out. So for ten minutes, we ate in the dark and laughed the entire time. I needed it.

On the return trip to the department for Jo's car, the police scanner sounded. The hairs on my arm stood to attention as I listened to the dispatcher announce, "officer down." Jo and I shared a glance. Then the dispatcher repeated the address, causing my heart to fall into my stomach.

"Jo, can you ride with me? I have to go to the scene." Without waiting for a reply, I activated my lights and sirens and sped past the department parking lot.

Jo realized there was no need to reply. "We didn't get called out to this one, Ryker. What's wrong?"

"This is Officer Hutton's case. I sent him to that address." I explained while I maneuvered around stopped cars. "Don't say it's not my fault." I could feel it coming.

She didn't and it wouldn't have mattered, anyway. The map's red circle flashes in front of my eyes because I circled it for Hutton. We skidded to a stop at the house's curb, and I was out the door before my car stopped rolling. I heard the ambulance pull in behind me as their tires skidded too.

Officer Hutton lay on the ground next to the house, holding his shoulder where blood seeped through his uniform. "Hutton, look at me." I snapped.

He opened his eyes. "Bartley, you came. We got all three of them. You did good." Then his teeth clenched as a ripple of pain pulsed through his body.

I grinned when I saw he would be okay. The ambulance attendants made me back away so they could reach the injured officer. They worked on him for a few minutes, then they loaded him onto a stretcher.

Hutton turned his head over his shoulder and yelled, "Bartley, I'll tell Madge you said hello." Then he giggled as the pain meds made their way to his bloodstream.

Jo walked over to me. "See, Bartley. Everything is fine. Hutton probably has a through and through bullet wound. Those heal quick." She rubbed my arm, and I looked at her.

She stands around 5'10," and Jo always wears jeans, a t-shirt, and a jacket. Today, she wore an emerald green shirt, and it made her eyes glow. Something I've never noticed before. Then her hairstyle is something she calls a pixie. It's bleach blonde, short, and sticks out in places, but it suits her.

When the ambulance left, we did too. I followed it until it turned right, heading to Madge's hospital. We turned into the lot, and I dropped Jo at her car. I thanked her for supper and for Hutton's scene. For all I know, I could've interrupted her plans.

I went home and contemplated going to the hospital to be there for Hutton. But then, I sat on the sofa and grew sleepy while I watched a baseball game. I woke long enough to turn off the television and make it to bed when I realized Madge hadn't made it home yet. Then I thought of Hutton again, before dozing off.

Madge came home around two in the morning. I always wake when I hear the doorknob rattle. It was a sign of entry, and for me, I needed to hear it. So, when she entered our bedroom, I asked about Hutton.

"He took a bullet to the shoulder, but he was lucky it missed the bones. He'll be out of work for a few days, but he'll be back in no time." Several minutes passed as Madge prepared for bed. I felt the bed move as she slid between the sheets. She was asleep within seconds.

The following day, Jo and I arrived at the same time. "No court for you today?" I asked, knowing how much she despises court.

"Nope. Thank goodness. Sitting in court is awful. I'm back with you." Jo smiled, and her eyes did that thing again. I tried not to notice.

We entered the division to a group of detectives huddled around someone's desk. Then I saw Greta standing at my desk with a blank face. When we got closer, she waved us to follow her. We bypassed our desks and entered Commander Huxley's office. She waited until we took our seats before closing the door.

"I have a recent case that I need your eyes on ASAP. Our dispatchers received a call requesting a welfare check at a home in an upscale neighborhood. Unfortunately, the responding officers found both homeowners deceased in the downstairs office."

Jo stared at Greta with a quizzical look. "What's so special about this one? Do we know the victims?"

"Someone killed them using a garrote."

I swallowed. "Did you say a garrote?" Instinctively, I reached up and touched my neck. Jo did the same. "This will be a first for me. I'm not sure I've heard of any other murders by garrote."

"We're checking our records now. The scene is active, so look at it while you can. Ryker, Jo, keep me in the loop on this one. Something feels different about it."

We stood as Greta handed me a slip of paper with an address printed on it. I'd know Greta's handwriting anywhere. I've never seen such perfect writing before. "We'll leave now and head to the scene."

On our way past our desks, we grabbed our notebooks. Neither of us knew what we would walk into, but listening to Greta, it sounded horrible. There's nothing like a gruesome crime scene before breakfast. We climbed into my car, and I drove us to the scene. Neither of us spoke.

I found a spot next to the curb, and I pulled in straight because there wasn't enough room to parallel park. Jo exited the car first, and she stared at me as my head cleared the car's roof. We nodded and made our way to the house.

On a scorching July day, an officer stood at the front door with a clipboard. No one goes in or out without signing the log. So once I slid booties on my feet, I stood and signed the log. Then I snapped gloves on my hands before I entered. After doing the same, Jo followed me inside. We saw no one but heard voices, so we turned and followed the voices. The scene stopped me in my tracks.

Two bodies remained. The man sat in his office chair with his head resting on his desk. The lady leaned against the side of the desk as she sat on the floor. Her head hung at an odd angle. Someone garroted both. It appeared their deaths occurred several days ago, but we haven't been told that. I guessed because of the stench and the body's condition. I studied the office, then I backed out.

Jo remained in the office, snapping photos. She was much better at that than I. I tried to read her face, but I couldn't. Her eyes remained steady as she photographed the victims and the office contents. When she finished, she found me in the kitchen. It baffled me. I couldn't see how the killer gained entry.

"Have you found the entry point, Bartley?" Jo asked because she knows I always search for an entry points.

"I'm guessing here." I pointed to the back door. "But I've found no evidence confirming it. I stepped out the door but found nothing inside or outside on the door frame or on the ground. I want to search the backyard before we leave. Did you hear anything while you were in the office?" I continued searching the area while I waited for a reply.

"No. The crime scene unit is waiting for the medical examiner. Their guess for the time of death is late Saturday night. One tech suggested the guy worked in his office into the early morning hours. Then the killer struck. The lady heard the commotion, came downstairs and faced her own death."

I nodded because it made sense. "As soon as they remove the bodies, we can get into the office. I want to see what's on the guy's desk." I reached for the door handle and pulled the door inward. As I stepped over the threshold for the second time, I studied the deck. Did I see a footprint? I reached my arm out, stopping Jo's progress.

"Look down there, Jo. Do you see a footprint?" I pointed to make sure she saw the area.

"Yea, there might be something there. I'm not sure it's a footprint, but it's something. We need to save it for the techs. I'll grab one." Jo turned and followed the path to the office. Seconds later, she returned with a tech in tow.

I showed him the area in question. He murmured something I didn't understand, but I didn't question him. While he worked, Jo and I inspected the backyard. The pool smelled of chlorine, and the air was fresh from the storms overnight. We found nothing in the flower beds or the pool house. But when I closed the door to the pool house, we spotted a missing panel in the privacy fence. This caused another picture to form. The missing board was large enough for a grown man to pass through. Now we needed to see the other side.

We climbed through the fence and entered into a park area. We exchanged a glance. This house was the perfect location for a crime scene. "Our killer does his homework before committing his crime. How many other murders has he committed?" I asked Jo as she surveyed the area.

"I can't fathom a guess. Greta said she felt something was off on this one. I agree with her. Are we looking at a serial killer, Ryker?" Jo played with her earring. That's her sign of trouble.

I shrugged my shoulders as a text alert sounded. "The medical examiner removed the bodies. Let's get a look at the guy's office." We turned and retraced our steps to the house. The park's image floated around in my mind as we entered the house. As we cross the threshold, I noticed the crime scene tech removed the marker at the back door.

Crime scene techs crawled through the house like spiders. They were everywhere, snapping pictures and logging information into their logbooks. When we entered the office, it sat empty. Pools of blood gathered on the desk and floor beside it. Jo headed for the desk while I searched the credenza and bookshelves.

"Ryker, this guy might be an attorney. He has legal documents spread across the desk. Did Greta give you the victim's names?" Jo asked with her head down.

"No, she didn't." I never turned to face Jo because I removed a book from the shelf and shook it, and there were tons of books on the shelves. Sometimes people hide things in books. We've solved several murders with information kept in a book. I gathered several business cards, a five-dollar bill, and a dry-cleaning receipt when I finished.

The duo continued inspecting the home office in silence as they pondered the reasons for the deaths. Finally, Jo, struggling to open a desk drawer, brought me back to the here and now. "Problems, Jo?"

"The guy must have locked this drawer. This is the only drawer with a lock, and I want to see inside." Jo huffed.

Just as she finished spouting off, an officer walked to the doorway, calling my name. "I'm Detective Ryker Bartley." I turned to face him. He looked maybe twenty years old, and his expression proves he's witnessed nothing like this before.

"Detective, Commander Huxley thought you might need this." He reached through the doorway with a paper in his hand. I took it and grinned. Greta is good.

"Thanks, Officer, for bringing it to us." The officer turned and left quickly, without glancing back.

Turning to Jo, "we have our warrant. Let me see what I can do with the drawer. Did you look for a key inside the middle desk drawer?" I walked over to the desk and studied the papers resting on top.

"I looked but found none. Here's a letter opener. It might help open the lock." Jo handed me the letter opener, and I dropped to my knees to see the lock. The lock was tiny, so I had no way of getting the opener inside. Instead of the lock, I slid the letter opener between the drawer and the desk and wrestled with it. I won when the lock popped.

The drawer opened, and files overflowed. These files were the attorney privilege kind. Client names graced the tops of the files with court dates printed in red. We needed a box for these many files. I faced Jo, and she grinned. "I knew we needed inside that drawer, but now our suspect list doubled." She stood from the desk chair and exited the room.

I read the names printed on the files. Some sounded familiar, while others didn't. This guy must be a well-known attorney. My eyes returned to the photos on the credenza. Then recognition strikes. "Hey, Jo. This guy knew the Governor. Here they are in a picture together at a formal event." Jo returned carrying a box for our files as she glanced over my shoulder.

"Swell. We know what that means for us." Jo stated as she placed the files inside the box. She barely had enough room to fit them in the box. As she laid the lid on top of the box, Jo glanced at the papers on the desk but opted to let them dry since blood-soaked them.

I picked up the tidbits I garnered from the books and tossed them on top of the box. When I faced the doorway, a light caught my attention. Closing the door, we noticed a security system keypad mounted to the wall. Jo and I studied it. The system appeared working, but did the homeowners activate it Saturday night? I jotted a note as a reminder to check with their monitoring service.

Once we completed the office search, we strolled the home, upstairs, and downstairs. The unwelcomed visitor left the other rooms untouched. As we headed across the catwalk to the other side, an officer exited the owner's suite, carrying a purse in one hand and a wallet in the other. "Detectives, the homeowners are Vernon and Eleanor Rivera. Her wallet confirms her name, as does the property tax assessor's office. I'll bag and tag this as evidence."

I thanked the officer for the information, and we returned downstairs. The visitor's entry still perplexed me. Did the visitor have a key? If not, how did he gain access without leaving marks on the door? "I want to check the garage door one more time. I'm struggling with the killer's entry technique." Jo followed me.

We scoured the doorframe and the floor, looking for a sign of entry. There was none. In fact, it looked as if the homeowners had recently painted the garage. Both vehicles sat in their parking spaces, too. So, if the intruder didn't come in the front, garage or back door, how did he do it?

"I'll retrieve our box and meet you at the car unless you want to see something else." I offered.

"I'm good to go, Ryker. But I'm hungry. I missed breakfast. What about you?" Jo grinned because she knew I could always eat. At 6'4", my frame takes a lot of food.

I sauntered off down the hall toward the office. As I meandered through the dining room, I checked every nook and cranny for evidence. I found none. So, I scooped the box from the floor and met Jo at the car. She had her head down, looking at her phone.

After I plopped the box in the back seat, she registered I was back. "Ryker, look at this. Vernon and Eleanor Rivera have gobs of articles written about them. Vernon is a high-powered injury lawyer, and his wife is also an attorney, but the articles mention no law firm for the wife. However, Vernon's firm is in downtown Fort Worth."

"I suggest we eat, then go to the office and make our plans. I'm sure Greta wants an update too." I slid into the driver's seat and waited until Jo buckled her seatbelt before I pulled away from the scene. "You pick lunch?"

Jo scrunched her nose because she had trouble deciding where to eat. But once she gets there, she knows what she wants. It's funny to watch her decide. Food has been her most complex decision since I've known her. "Just drive through a burger place. That's the easiest." I chuckled.

A few miles closer to town, I turn into a drive-thru, and we order. Since these burgers can be messy, I pull the car under a shade tree, and we eat and talk. We still have no viable reasons for the deaths of Vernon and Eleanor. Robbery wasn't the motive with the cash, jewelry and cars still at the home. Jo asked about Eleanor and Vernon's relationship. Was one or the other having an affair? That could be a reason for the murders.

I glanced at Jo as she swallowed her last bite of her double cheeseburger. "Who do you know can discuss a gruesome murder scene over a hamburger meal?" We laugh at that one.

"Ryker, we can eat and talk murder all day. You should know that by now." We share another glance, and her eyes do that thing again. I have to break the spell, so I start the car and turn out of the lot before glancing at Jo again.

Greta stands at our desks when we enter the office. I place the box on my desk and follow Greta to her office. We spend an hour discussing the case and the victims. Greta knew Vernon, but she didn't say how. Her face turned red when we told her we couldn't find an entry point. Then she excused us from her office.

Jo looked over at me and mumbled, "She must have known Vernon more than she's willing to share."

I didn't reply. Sometimes it's better to stay quiet, especially around women. While I sorted Vernon's files, Jo ordered the backgrounds of each victim. She reviewed them, then gave me the rundown, which was short. Neither person has a police record, not even a traffic ticket. They have enough money in the bank to do whatever they want.

Sitting in my chair, I asked, "Was this an opportunity murder or premeditated? I'm leaning to premeditated. The killer knew how to enter the premises without detection. No one would know that unless they surveilled the house."

Jo's head bobbed as she rehashed my sentiment. "The motive remains unclear to me. Why would someone kill this couple? Could an unhappy client have killed Vernon and Eleanor walked in on it?"

"Anything is possible. Do you know if the crime scene techs found our victims' cell phones or laptops?"

Plucking a piece of paper from her desk, Jo read the list of evidence collected from the scene. "Two cell phones and two laptops are sitting in the lab, along with a host of other personal items. It doesn't appear the killer took anything when he left. So, were the murders just for fun?"

A niggle creeps up my spine as I consider Jo's remarks. What kind of person kills two people with a garrote for fun? Killing someone with a garrote is personal, similar to drowning someone. You are close to the victim when they take their final breath. "Have there been any other murders using a garrote?"

Jo clicked a few keys on the keyboard and swung her head from side to side. "I think we would have heard about it if there was. Who's ever heard of using a garrote to murder someone? I haven't, and I've been in law enforcement since I graduated high school." She saw me grin, and she pointed at me. "Don't even make a snide comment about my age. You're right there with me."

We joke about our ages because she is thirty-seven days, two hours, and five minutes older than me. During that time, I have the pleasure of calling her the older woman, and when I do, she acts mad, but I know she isn't. It's a fun thirty-seven days, two hours, and five minutes for me, anyway.

The day ends just like it started with more questions than answers. I didn't ask Jo about her supper plans.

Instead, I went home alone because I needed to think.

Chapter 2

I sat in our home office, studying street maps of the murder location. The Rivera's home sits in a swanky neighborhood of the well-to-do. Their home borders a park giving easy access to the backyard, but how many people know this? I hadn't a clue until we found the missing board. Did the Rivera's know their fence had a missing board? While this neighborhood has no front gates, our department has had few police reports. This brings me back to the security system panel behind the office door. That issue is at the top of the list for tomorrow.

At 9:00 pm., Madge entered the house. She looked exhausted, but she smiled when I peeked out of the office. I stood and walked to her. She reached up for a hug, and I provided one. We stood in silence for a while before breaking away. Finally, Madge asked, "why are you in the office at this time of night?"

"I didn't hear from you, so I waited until you called or came home. And we have a case involving a well-known attorney." I hate when she asks me questions about open cases, but this one is all over the news, anyway.

With her head nodding, she says, "I saw that on the news a few hours ago. Is it true someone killed Vernon and Eleanor with a garrote?" She rubbed her neck as she waited for my reply.

"Unfortunately, it's true. It's a strange case too. I'm going to bed now that you're home. Are you coming?"

Madge replied, "I'll be there shortly. I need to eat since I missed supper."

With that comment, I went to bed and fell asleep, never hearing Madge join me. The following day was stifling hot when I parked my car in the lot. Our summer weather is pleasant one day, and the next is humid while we wait for the storms. With today's humidity, the storms weren't too far behind.

Jo beat me into the office today. She already had coffee sitting on my desk. I could see the steam rising and smell the aroma as I got closer. This was special coffee from her favorite shop. I grinned as I couldn't wait for my first sip. It's been a while since I've experienced the flavor.

With the coffee's heat and the flavors sliding over my tongue, all of my shoulder tension eased. I woke with knots lining my shoulders, and nothing I did seemed to soothe them until now. How did Jo know? We glanced at the other. She gave me a chance to enjoy the first few sips before she started.

"Good morning to you, too. We have a meeting with the attorneys at Vernon Rivera's office at 9:30. Did you call the security company to verify if their system is operational?" Jo inquired as she read a note from her book.

I pulled my list from my pocket and unfolded it, and pointed to it as I explained, "I'll do that now." I leaned over, lifted the phone to my ear, and dialed a number for the security system company. Jo watched and listened as I spoke to the day manager. When I ended the call, I gave Jo the news. "The security system is operational. The Rivera's turned it on at 9:00 pm and then turned it off around midnight on the night of the murder. It's been off since then."

Jo's eyebrows bunched together. "That seems odd. Did Vernon have an appointment with someone, or did he step out to his car for something and forget to arm the system again?"

"I don't recall seeing a calendar on Vernon's desk. Maybe he used his phone or computer for his planning. Let's head over to the attorney's office. That will take most of the day."

We gathered our notes and walked outside into the sweltering heat again. At least today, we'll spend it indoors interviewing Vernon's workmates. While I don't expect to learn anything earth-shattering, it's still part of the investigation process.

The attorneys and their staff gathered in the massive conference room. They carried solemn expressions, and some appeared nervous. It could be they've never spoken to a detective, much less worked with a murdered victim.

I introduced us to the group, then gave some preliminary instructions on how their day would unfold. We started with the firm's partners. There were two remaining.

Neither partner had anything negative to say about Vernon Rivera. Vernon made partner ten years ago, and he was instrumental in the firm's growth. There had been no threats against the firm or Vernon. However, they agreed to review his cases, and if anything transpired, they would notify us.

Next, we spoke with each attorney assigned to the firm. Again, we learned nothing of interest. Everyone seemed to love Vernon. He was an exceptional trial lawyer and teacher as he worked with the firm's younger attorneys.

Our last interview of the day was with Talia, Vernon's assistant. When she entered the conference room, we noticed her red-rimmed eyes. Jo spoke first. "Talia, thanks for coming in to meet us. We need a little background on Vernon, and we hope you can help."

Talia sat at the table with her hands in her lap. When Jo said Vernon's name, Talia brought a tissue to her face and dabbed at her eyes. "I'm sorry, I can't stop the tears. What do you need to know?"

Jo asked about the workload, his family life and any disagreements with co-workers. Talia described the workload as heavy, but that's expected in an active law firm. Then she confirmed there had been no disagreements with any co-workers. Finally, the one statement that stuck out was that Eleanor wanted children, but Vernon didn't. Eleanor gave up her practice to stay at home while they tried to conceive a child because she feared the job stress prevented her from conceiving. Once she had been away from the job for a while and was still not pregnant, she gave up the idea of being a mother. So, she started her own home for unwed mothers. It's still open today.

Talia's statement closed the door on the interviews. I knew we'd find nothing at the law firm. Once Talia exited the room, I glanced at Jo and asked, "who would kill a perfect couple, and why?"

Jo had no answer for me, so she shook her head as she gathered our notes from the table. Finally, I spoke with the receptionist, advising her of our departure. She grinned and stared at me as we left. Then Jo stated, "Ryker, I think she adores you."

"Who?" I replied, knowing the answer already. Then I chuckled.

With a headshake, "really, Ryker? The girl behind the desk. She studied you from head to toe." Jo looked at me, and her eyes were dark. Was she jealous?
"I didn't pay her attention. She was way too young for me." I tried to play it cool because I couldn't read Jo's attitude.

We worked through lunch, so we were starving by the time we climbed into my car. "So, how does it feel to have wasted an entire day? We learned nothing of value. Everyone loved Vernon and Eleanor Rivera." I stated, but it was more for me than anyone else.

"You know how I feel about wasting time. This day made me angrier that someone felt the need to murder these people. These people are the kind we need on the earth, so they can do good things. Instead. some low life ended it for them." Jo reached up and played with her earring.

Patting her arm, I stated, "We'll get the person who murdered them. We always do." I pulled away from the law firm and drove to a nearby eatery. Over the next thirty minutes, we devoured our food while deciding on our next step.

Once we returned to the solitude of the car, Jo asked, "what are your thoughts, Ryker? I see no reason for the Rivera's deaths. Not one person had a negative comment against them."

"Someone had a reason for killing them, and we must find it. The crime lab should be forthcoming with details of their findings soon. If we're lucky, they'll provide the evidence we can use." But even after I said it, I didn't believe it because I agreed with Greta that this case felt different from the others. I couldn't explain it, but something stirred in me when I compared this case to others we've worked.

By the time we returned to the office, the parking lot had cleared. We rolled into a spot at the door. As we entered, the day shift officers were exiting, and after a brutally hot day, they were ready to head home and cool off because another hot day would follow.

Jo walked to the desk while I stopped for coffee. I needed something to help me think. Today was monotonous, as one person after another told us how great the Rivera's were. If someone is so great, why kill them? They obviously made someone mad, but who?

While walking to my desk, I answered Madge's call. Jo chuckled when she saw me with a phone in one hand and coffee in the other. Madge called to inform me of another late night. One of her scheduled nurses has a sick child. I struggled to put two words together. This was becoming commonplace between us, and our lives seemed to move in opposite directions. Madge knew this troubled me, but yet it happened repeatedly. This night I was free. She wasn't, and vice versa. The call ended with the obligatory be safe comment.

As I sat, Jo stared at me. She leaned toward me as our desk faced. "What's going on, Ryker? And don't tell me nothing."

"Now isn't the time. I'll let you know when I know." I gave her a slight grin, then I leaned back in my chair and sipped my coffee. It wasn't as good as Jo's exceptional coffee, but it's hot and liquid.

I opened my notebook and scanned my notes. Nothing new here. Next, I reviewed Jo's scene photos and compared them to the photos from the crime scene techs. Again, they told us the same thing. The Rivera's were tidy people. Everything had a place. Vernon's occupation was the only area of concern, and even that hasn't produced a lead.

"Jo, this case is a dead end. Did the uniform officers canvas the neighbors? I don't see where they have uploaded their information yet." I asked as I scrolled through the report on my laptop.

Jo's head swung from side to side. "Their report is due today. I know one officer works the night shift this week. Maybe they'll upload tonight for us."

Standing from my desk, "feel like a repeat for supper? I'm on my own again," Asking with a head tilt and a grin.

I waited through a brief hesitation before Jo replied, "sure, sounds good." The strange part was her eyes focused on the floor, not on me.
We enjoyed dinner at my favorite sports bar. They have the best wings in town. Jo opted for a burger while I ate basket after basket of wings. They played the baseball game on multiple screens. We

ate, talked, and watched sports. I couldn't believe a woman would sit through dinner like this. This was the best night I've had in a long time, and I thanked Jo for it. Then her eyes danced.

Thank goodness we drove separately to dinner. It made escaping her eyes easier. The house was dark when I entered, and I went to bed without wondering about Madge.

The following day was a scorcher. On the way into the office, you could see the heat ripples bounce up from the pavement. Unfortunately, the air conditioner in my police-issued vehicle couldn't keep up with my demand. When I arrived at the office, I slid from my seat, slammed my car door, and trotted into the building, expecting cold air. But I got the opposite. Instead, it was stifling hot inside the office.

I wandered my way to my desk when I noticed the investigations division sat empty. Maybe the heat ran them away. Hearing a commotion, I glanced at the door. Greta entered, followed by a service repair tech. She spoke low but authoritative. He nodded but didn't speak. When he left, she approached me.

"Ryker, anything new on the Rivera's murder? I hear there isn't much evidence."

"We have no evidence. There were no visible signs of entry, and everyone loved the victims. The crime lab hasn't forwarded their results yet, but we aren't expecting any help." I stated as I shrugged my shoulders.

"Keep me updated on changes. The Governor called me yesterday wanting a status report. You know how that rolls, Ryker." Greta spoke with a subtle undercurrent.

I nodded in acknowledgment. Then I asked the obvious, "any idea how long we'll be without air?"

Greta looked at me, turned on her high heels, walked to her office, and closed the door. She's just as miserable as the rest of us.

Sweat beaded on my upper lip, and it ran down the sides of my face. It's too hot to think. I texted Jo about her status. She just parked in the lot. I returned the text by saying, "stay there. On my way to you."

In seconds, I had unplugged my laptop, grabbed my notebook, and stepped into the stairwell. There was no need to risk the elevator in this heat. Jo's car sat idling, so I slid into the passenger seat. "Why are you sweaty?" Jo asked with a scrunched nose.

"The office is without air condition. It's too hot to breathe in there. I brought my laptop and notes. Take us somewhere we can review what we have."

Jo backed out of the lot, and we landed at her favorite coffee place. I grinned, as I should have known. We ordered drinks and muffins. Then we took to a corner table. We discussed in low voices what we knew about Rivera's case. Unfortunately, the neighborhood canvas notes were not available yet. Not that we expected anything from it.

My cell phone blared in my pocket. I answered a call from our dispatcher as they dispatched us to a home invasion call not too far from our current location. We calmed when the dispatcher confirmed the perpetrators escaped capture.

With lights and sirens, Jo cut through traffic in record time. One patrol car sat in the drive while the other skidded to a stop at the curb. We parked at the curb because the ambulance took the remaining space in the driveway.

A uniform officer greeted us at the front door after he escorted the EMTs to the homeowner. We wanted a chance to speak with the homeowner, but that would come with a trip to the hospital. Jo veered off to the kitchen area in search of the victim while I spoke with the officer. The officer described the scene upon his arrival. He was first to the location, and as he stated on his approach to the victim's house, he heard her screaming. He thought someone was still inside with her, but that turned out to be false.

Once the victim realized the officers were legit, she let them enter the house. The homeowner described the perpetrators as young guys, one white and one

Latino. Both wore red bandannas around their neck. The white guy had short brown hair, while the Latino guy had dark medium-length hair. The Latino guy asked her for her name. When she answered, they looked at each other, said a few curse words, and stormed out of the house. They drove a sports vehicle with a loud muffler. It might be a Mustang, but she isn't good with car models.

"Great job on the interview. Was she alone at the time of the assault?" I asked as I jotted a few more notes in my book.

"Yes, Detective, she was alone. She mentioned dropping her kids at school." The officer explained after referencing his report.

Jo returned and nodded her head to step outside. I followed. "This is another weird one. The homeowner was pistol-whipped three times to the side of her head. There is blood, but not a lot. The victim said the perpetrators left the scene when she told them her name."

"That's the same story I got from the officer." The ambulance crew pushed through the front door, so we stopped talking. We watched them roll her to the rig. One EMT turned to us and said they would take her to the downtown hospital. I rolled my eyes. "My question is simple. Was this a botched home invasion? Did the guys enter the wrong house? If so, the actual victim sits in waiting."

Since there wasn't anything to see at the house, we followed the ambulance to the hospital. Maybe they would let us speak with the victim before they stitched her head. Neither of us spoke as we drove to the hospital. What's the odds of getting weird assignments within days of each other?

By the time we parked and entered the ER, the ambulance deposited the victim. Jo and I walked into the ER searching for a nurse when a doctor walked from an exam room. We showed our badges, then I asked about our victim. He pointed to the space he vacated and said, "she's in there if you want to speak with her. We haven't started stitching her head yet."

I heard my name, and when I turned, I saw Madge approaching. Jo stepped to the side as if to take a call, leaving me with my wife. Madge asked, "what brings you by here?"

"A home invasion and the homeowner was pistol-whipped. She's in there waiting for stitches." I pointed to the exam room. Before Madge answered, someone paged her to the trauma unit, and she was off without a glance back.

Jo watched the scene play out, but she never commented. She knows there's trouble in paradise. It must be apparent. I didn't offer an explanation. Instead, I walked into our victim's room.

The homeowner had gauze wrapped around her head, stemming the blood flow, but not entirely as a trickle inched its way down her neck to her hospital gown. She didn't seem to notice, and we didn't point it out. Jo stepped closer to the bed than me, and she asked the questions. Our victim described her encounter as freaky. The guys left her home when she told them her name. She got the impression they knew they were in the wrong house. Jo and I shared a glance as we confirmed this version matches what she told the officer earlier.

Jo asked what time the incident occurred. The victim stated she returned home from grocery shopping after dropping her kids at school. She guesses about 11:00 am. We asked if she recognized either guy, and she exclaimed, "NO!" When the doctor returned, we left because she couldn't tell us anything new. And we didn't want to watch the show.

Neither spoke as we headed back to the car. Once inside, Jo looks at me, "if these guys hit the wrong house, we have another one that's a sitting duck." She shook her head, then suggested, "can you look at the map and determine their next stop? Then we can send undercover patrols to the area."

I agreed with Jo, but only to keep her quiet. With her driving, I needed to think not only about the case but about my marriage. Could we save our marriage, or is it too far gone? Could I find the next area for this home invasion duo? There were too many questions.

We entered the office to a blast of cold air. It felt good as it dried my sweat. Jo pulled a mutilated street map from her desk that looked older than either of us. She pointed to the house from the home invasion. "What's the street number?" I asked as I studied the map.

"It's 2105."

After scouring the map, I returned to my laptop. I toyed with a few queries, then I stated, "there are two other 2105's within three blocks of her house. We need to notify the patrol. Maybe one of the other's looks similar to our victim's. If so, I'd start with that one." Jo stared at me as I spoke. Once I finished, she called patrol and talked to the duty sergeant.

While Jo spent time on the phone, I pulled our notes from the law firm. Nothing struck me as notable, but I didn't want to discount anything either. Just as I spread the file open across my desk, my phone rang. I answered and listened to the crime lab tech burst my bubble for the second time today. I took notes because I had to recount the conversation with Jo and Greta. When my call ended, I felt Jo's eyes staring at me.

She asked, "please tell me that's good news?"

"I wouldn't call it good news, but it's news, nonetheless. There was no DNA found in the Rivera house. The shoe print from the back desk was useless. There are still working on the cell phones while the laptop offered nothing." I glanced at my notes to make sure I overlooked nothing.

"That's it? That's all the lab gave us. We have nothing, no leads, no suspects." Jo twisted her earring as she pondered the lack of results.

I studied the pictures again. How did the killer enter the house? Was the killer a friend? "This was a calculated and precise murder. I think they've killed before. What's the likelihood of a first-time murderer leaving no DNA?" I tilted my head as I glanced at Jo, waiting for a reply.

"Now, that's a scary thought, Ryker. But we found no other murders with a garrote. How do you explain that?" Jo countered.

"I don't, yet. Unless he changes his killing method." I added the last comment as an afterthought, but the more I considered it, the more it felt right. I lifted my eyes from the photos, and Jo nodded in agreement.

Jo stood and moved behind me, so she viewed the pictures too. She moved a few around on my desk. "I think you might be onto something, Ryker. This kill wasn't messy. The killer contained the blood in the office, but how did he keep it off of his shoes?

He should have had some blood from the second kill." She pointed to the blood pool on the carpet. "See right here. How did he not have blood on his shoes?"

When Jo pointed to it, I grabbed my magnifying glass from my middle drawer and held it in front of my right eye. "I see it now. There is a smudge next to the blood pool on the floor. But I'm unsure if it's from a shoe or the lady. If the killer moved her to that position, the movement might have caused the smudge." Then I had another thought, "he might have worn booties too. If he did, he wore them until he was safely away from the scene, then he tossed them."

"Do we share your thoughts about the murder with Greta?" Jo asked with an eyebrow lifted.

"Let's think on it before we drop that bombshell," I suggested.

Since we had decisions to make, we left the office at a decent time today. I texted Madge to check her schedule, and she got off in thirty minutes. We'll meet at the house and decide on dinner. I was ready for the talk.

I made it home before I received a text from Greta stating she reassigned our home invasion case because she wanted our attention on the Rivera murder. Greta gave me a 9:00 am meeting time to discuss the Rivera case. That's not a lot of time for significant decisions. I quickly sent Jo a message with the updates. She sent me a thumbs up for a reply.

Checking the clock for the umpteenth time, I grew more frustrated and hungrier. Madge hasn't bothered to call or text about her delayed arrival. This is always how it is with us. I gave in and sent a text. Then I waited to see the three dots bounce on the screen. After five minutes, I caved.

In a spur-of-the-moment decision, I texted Jo, asking her to meet to discuss the case. I had my answer in thirty seconds and was driving to the halfway point between our houses. She made it to the restaurant before me. I couldn't tell who was more anxious.

I devoured my food while she picked at hers. Something troubled her, and it wasn't the case. Jo never said. So, we discussed the case using paper napkins. Each napkin was a plausible scenario. By the time we ran out of ideas, we knew we had to tell Greta the idea.

We said our goodnights in the parking lot. Jo acted as if she had more to say, but she didn't. I couldn't take any more emotional trials right now. My marriage teeters on the edge of collapse, and I need to resolve it one way or the other.

While I was at supper with Jo, Madge texted me, saying she would be late, and she was sorry. Same story, different day. I acknowledged the text with a sad face because I had no words. At that moment, I decided to live my life, and when the time came for us to talk, we would.

I unloaded the napkins onto my bathroom counter as I prepared for bed. Out of the scenarios we discussed, the most plausible is the killer changing his method. Or Jo suggested the killer might be from another part of the country, and he's moved into our area. With that idea, the FBI would have alerted the department to a potential killer in the area, but only if they knew where he moved.

When I woke the following day, Madge was asleep beside me. I shook my head because that bothered me. The doorknob rattle didn't wake me. I guess I needed the rest. I slipped from the bed, showered, and made it into the kitchen before I heard Madge's footsteps heading to the shower. If she hurried, we could start our talk this morning before work.

Madge spoke with someone on the phone as she took the steps downstairs. It sounded like a hospital call. I cringed because I feared another escape. This time, she shocked me. She described her night. A hospital surgeon had a heart attack while performing surgery. They worked on him for a long time, but he died around 2:00 am and the surgery patient is fine.

"That's awful. I've never thought of anything like that happening," expressing my concern because it threw me a loop this morning.

"I'm on my way back to the hospital to take his place today until we can fill his spot in the rotation." She grabbed a banana and kissed me on the cheek, then turned when she made it to the door. "See you later, okay."

She shut the door before I could answer. I turned to the counter with my mind numb. My coffee turned cold, and my stomach queasy. So, I gathered my napkins and drove to the office.

As I entered the office building, my mind returned to yesterday and no air conditioning. The temps were already hot, and I couldn't imagine how brutal the afternoon would turn. I braced for the worst, but a frigid blast hit my face as I crossed the threshold. Well, at least the air worked. I grinned for the first time today.

Jo sat at her desk, studying something on the laptop, when she saw me. She closed her computer, picked her notebook up, and met me halfway to Greta's. "Are we ready to tell her your idea? I made some queries this morning about unsolved in our area. There aren't as many as I thought. I found three or four that would be worth a second look."

"Good to know. You can share that information with Greta." We took a few more steps when Jo touched my arm.

"Are you okay, Ryker? You look upset." Jo asked in her soft voice.

"I'm fine. Just marital woes, I guess. Come on, Jo. Greta's waiting." I turned, walking to Greta's office as Jo followed. I felt her eyes on my back.

Greta held her favorite red coffee cup to her lips when we stepped into her office. When she lowered the cup, she sported a powdered sugar mustache. "Enjoy the donut, Greta?" I chuckled as she tried to wipe away the evidence.

Jo joined, "where's the box?" She can't pass on a donut. They should be a food group for her.

Greta slid the box to the desk's edge, and we plucked a freshly baked donut from the box. The smell made my stomach flip, reminding me I failed to eat breakfast. I chose a plain donut while Jo enjoyed a frosted chocolate one. Greta gave us a few minutes to indulge our senses before the meeting began.

Greta stood from her chair and walked to her office door. When she closed it, I knew she meant business. It's time to tell her my theory. She returned to her chair and stared at us. Then Jo turned to me.

"The latest information came from the crime lab. They offered us nothing. No DNA from the crime scene. The shoe print was useless, but they continued to work on the cell phones. Apparently, Vernon had encrypted their cell phones. We assume because of his work. Their laptops proved no reason for the murders either. We have zero evidence and zero threats against both victims." I stopped, waiting for a question.

"Ryker, what are your thoughts? I know you and Jo have discussed the case." Greta asked.

I pulled the napkins from my notebook, and she chuckled. After I laid them across her desk, I pointed to my theory. She read the napkin, then glanced from me to Jo. "You think the killer is a practiced murderer?" Greta inquired with skepticism.

"Yes, I do. The scene was too clean. No first-time killer leaves a scene that clean. There is always something to leave behind, hair or fiber. This scene left no physical evidence. There wasn't even a sign of forced entry." The information left Greta speechless. And that doesn't happen often.

Then she glanced at us, "do we have any unsolved murders involving a garrote?"

"No." We answered in unison, sharing a glance.

We turned our heads to face Greta and watched her head tilt and eyebrow lift. "Well? There must be more."

Over the next few hours, I shared my killer theory using different methods of murdering people. He might use a gun, knife or suffocation. But since the killer thinks he's smarter than us, he continues his murder spree using whatever method he chooses. He believes if he uses different techniques, we won't suspect the same person committed multiple murders.

"I have to admit, I've never considered one killer with different methods of killing. Most killers stay with the same method. Wonder why this one would change his method?" Greta doodled on her paper as she considered my theory.

Jo looked at me, and we turned our heads to Greta. She didn't offer an idea or a comment as she doodled. But you knew she was thinking because while doodling with her right hand, she twisted the ring on her left index finger.

After a couple of minutes of silence, Greta faced us. "I need time to digest this information. It's the best theory I've heard. I've never worked on a killer who changes methods, and I'd like to consider it a little longer. Thanks, guys. You two always deliver." That was our cue to leave, and we did after we plucked another donut from the box.

Since our mouths were full, we walked to our desk without speaking. On the way, I wondered if Greta believed our theory. The more I worked on the scenario, the more I did. Some guy picked random people to try new killing techniques just to see if it works. That brought another question. Are the victims random?

Chapter 3

Jo sat across from me and watched as I savored every bite of my blueberry donut. Then I sipped my coffee, and together, that was scrumptious. I patted my lips with my napkin, then I saw her staring at me.

"What? Did I miss a spot?"

With a round of laughter, "no, you didn't miss a spot, but you sure enjoyed those donuts. I don't think I've ever seen you eat so many at one time."

As I thought back, Jo was right. I rarely eat so many donuts at a sitting. "I couldn't help it. So, what do you think Greta will say about our theory?"

Jo paused before she answered. "She'll agree with you. If she does, Greta will pull any cold case files we have, then she'll pull from other departments. This could be monumental."

"While we wait, I suggest we return to the Rivera's neighborhood to poke around. I also want to check out the park behind their house. We might find nothing, but it's worth a try."

"Let's do it before Greta slaps us behind a desk." Jo stood as she spoke. She plucked her notebook from the stack of files on her desk, waiting on me because neither of us favors paperwork. "Talk to me about the killing methods. Do you think the killer shoots people too?"

"He could also suffocate, drown, or stab, too. There are many methods of murder. I've heard some murderers stage killings to favor accidents. If the theory comes to fruition, this will take some figuring out. It will take some doing to determine how he picks his victims and where they take place. They have involved me in nothing like this since I joined the department."

Jo smiled, then commented, "I've been doing this job longer than you, and I've worked nothing like it before, either. The good news is cases like this don't happen often."

We walked out into the Texas summer heat. Then I questioned my idea of poking around Rivera's neighborhood and the park. With the temps rising, maybe it will be a quick stop. I looked at Jo to see if she thought the same. She didn't. She faced straight ahead, heading to the car while I wondered if my shoe soles would melt before I reached it.

With the air conditioning turned on high, the car's temp was stifling. It took several miles before sweat stop running down my back. "Want to try the neighborhood first? It didn't look too active the other day, so I can't imagine today being any different."

When I heard nothing, I glanced at Jo. Her head bobbed, but she offered no words. I didn't push, but I felt she was working on something. She'd shared when she was ready.

We cruised through the Rivera's neighborhood. Again, all was quiet. No kids playing and no one doing yard work. Was it the neighborhood or the weather that kept people inside? When we passed the Rivera's home, crime scene tape fluttered against the front door. The next door neighbors already had a for sale sign in their yard, but you would've thought crime scene tape a deterrent for a home sale.

Jo's eyes followed mine. "That's awkward. Wonder how the Realtor explains the crime scene tape? They should have waited before placing the sign in the yard." Jo shook her head at the ramifications of murder.

I circled back to the entrance, then we followed another road to the park. We found a space under a shade tree, and the temps dropped ten degrees. This is obviously where the neighborhood folks come to walk. We saw more people here than in the neighborhood. I felt hopeful.

We split since we wanted to speak with as many people as possible. I blocked a runner, and he wasn't happy. After I explained my reason, he calmed, but his legs continued pumping. He lives in the same neighborhood as the Rivera's, but he knew nothing of their death. I let him return to jogging since it's hard to talk to someone bouncing.

Next, I sat on a bench with a mom as her children played on the swings. She was polite and concerned for her family's safety. I sympathized with her as I asked her questions. She told me what I didn't want to hear. People use this park all day, every day. Workers and delivery people eat lunch and take their breaks here. The park is vast as it continues around on the far side and borders another neighborhood.

Jo stood next to a jungle gym as she spoke with a lady. The lady tried to talk with Jo and keep her eyes on a boy and a girl. The boy ran from one plaything to another while the girl walked over to her mom. I watched as Jo kneeled and spoke to the little girl. Then Jo pulled her badge from her waist and let the little girl hold it. The boy saw the exchange, and he joined them for a touch, too. I never realized Jo was so good with kids until now. The little girl handed Jo her badge, then they hugged. When Jo stood, she turned, and we locked eyes. There's that thing again.

I looked at my phone, hoping for a reason to answer. There wasn't one. As I returned my gaze, Jo headed in my direction. We needed to share our finds, which wasn't much for me. Other than many people use this park. I made a mental note to check on surveillance cameras, even though I didn't spot any when we entered.

We walked to the car and leaned against it to rehash our visits. After discussing our encounters, we decided the killer knew about the park or found it during the Rivera's surveillance. There was no way he could've pulled off the murders without prior surveillance. He knew the ins and outs of the house and the occupants.

Our next stop would be lunch, then once we made it back to the office, we would check into the Rivera's deliveries. We might get lucky and find out a delivery person caused their deaths.

Just as we settled in the car, my phone rang. The caller requested us to stop by the crime lab. The Rivera's cell phone is operational. My interest peeked. "Change of plans. The crime lab requested a visit. They have the Rivera's cell phones ready for inspection."

"Let's do that first, then we can eat. I'm hoping the phones give us a clue, maybe from their contacts or calendars." Jo offered, then looked out the window.

I didn't reply because I concentrated on my search for cameras. Jo noticed my actions. "If you're looking for cameras, there aren't any. One of the park discussions confirmed the park doesn't have cameras."

"Everything about this case is a roadblock. Here's to hoping the cell phones offer a lead."

The rest of the trip was quiet because we digested what we heard from the park folks. Later, we entered the lab in a rush of cold air. Their workplace was always colder than the rest of the building. Our tech met us at the door, granting entry.

"Come back here, Detectives. The phones are on another counter." The lab tech instructed.

We entered an adjoining room, and electronics covered every inch of the space. I assumed someone uses these gadgets, but I wouldn't have any idea where to start. Finally, the tech lifted Vernon's phone from the counter. "This is Mr. Rivera's. There are calendar appointments during the week, one after the other. He worked from eight in the morning until around five, with a few meetings lasting into the early evening. Mr. Rivera played golf twice a week. He didn't mention the location of the course, but there was a contact for a country club. I've printed his calendar for you. Next are his contacts. There are over two thousand on the phone. Some contacts had Mr. Rivera's personal notations with the name. I've also printed those."

I couldn't fathom knowing over two thousand people. How did he meet them? While I'm sure some were clients, were the other people friends? That sounds like an overabundance to me.

The tech moved on to Eleanor's phone. "Mrs. Rivera was heavily into volunteering. She also filled her calendar with volunteer opportunities and spent a lot of time at her home for unwed mothers. She had just as many contacts as Vernon. I've highlighted the contacts that showed for both phones. Eleanor had three different nightly events that Vernon didn't attend, or at least they weren't on his calendar. Two were for her home for unwed mothers, which she calls E's Home, and one for another volunteer organization."

Jo directed a question to the tech, "did either phone show household deliveries?"

"None that I saw. Here are the printouts for both phones. Sorry, it's so much paper. I didn't know the depth these people carried in the community. I hope you find the person responsible for their deaths." The tech escorted us from the room as we each held onto a half ream of paper.

We walked to my car with so many thoughts in our heads, we opted not to talk. Do we concentrate on people that are on both phones? Or the events where Vernon didn't attend? Would that angle be a waste of time?

Jo sighed when she closed the car door. With the stack of paper on her lap, she thumbed through the pages. "This is a lot of information. I bet the lab tech had to add ink to his printer when he finished with our order."

I laughed. "You're probably right. What are your thoughts on this recent information?"

"I'm unsure where to begin. With so many contacts, it could take weeks or a month to track down every person on these phones, and that's with help. We haven't received a new assignment since this case hit our board. Is that a coincidence?"

I shook my head as I turned right. My goal is to eat lunch, then I'd worry about the next steps. After eating those donuts, I promised myself a trip to the gym. I hadn't been in days, and I could feel it. With this job, you can't afford to feel sluggish.

Jo runs for her exercise. She amazes me because she runs without a clear destination. Then, when her heart rate and pulse are where she wants them, she returns to her starting place. I've seen her leave the office in running clothes. Jo claims running empties her mind and gives her a chance to work through scenarios. For me, I'd have to concentrate on maintaining my stride. If too much clouded my mind, I'd fall flat on my face.

"Where should we eat? I'm considering a chicken salad for lunch." I offered as I took another corner.

Jo chuckled. "Too many donuts, Ryker? I wondered how long it would take before they bothered you."

"I'll admit I haven't been to the gym in days, but I've promised myself a trip today," I explained as I turned into a fast-food restaurant lot, and Jo's facial expression was priceless. "Why that look? This place has a great grilled chicken salad. Come on." I stepped from the car, and before I reached the door, sweat dropped from my brow.

Over lunch, we discussed the Rivera's case by rehashing everything. Even with the stacks of papers, we lacked direction. For lack of anything better, we opted to speak with the non-shared contacts first. Then we would reconvene.

We sat at our desk after lunch, combing the lists for the outliers. The lab tech helped since he highlighted those for us. With the lengthy list, it took time to complete the task. At 3:00 pm, my cell phone rang. It was Greta. I answered, and she asked for our location. When I told her we sat at our desks, she asked to see us.

Jo stood, "here we go, Ryker. This could be huge."

We entered Greta's office and took a seat. Her face was unreadable, so we waited for instruction. Greta reassigned us, so we were off the board for new cases. When she said that, I knew we were in for the most significant case of our careers.

"Now that you have no new cases coming your way, I'm placing you on a temporary assignment. The evidence room is sending all unsolved murder cases to you. From what I know, there are three in Fort Worth. Once you examine these, I want a detailed report outlining your evidence and thoughts if this is the same killer. Time is of the essence here. The captain approved this move, but he doesn't want you two dragging out the investigation. If you can't say the same killer murdered these victims, then we move on. We'll circle back to the Rivera's and try another tactic. Questions?" Greta's explanation rang clear to me.

Neither of us had a question. We knew our parameters, and we knew we wouldn't succeed sitting across from Greta. Standing, she stated, "let's follow the evidence. Report to me as soon as possible." We nodded.

Returning to our desks, the monumental task before us hit me. What would the unsolved cases prove? Do we have a serial killer lurking in our streets?

Since the boxes didn't arrive by 5:00 pm, we left. I headed for the gym, and Jo jogged out the front door, heading downtown Fort Worth. She claimed she enjoyed running along the busy streets as people tried to get home at a decent hour.

The gym was just what I needed to clear my head. When I walked outside, the humidity caused another round of sweat to break out all over my body. Once home, I parked in the garage then I walked back to the mailbox sitting at the end of our drive. On my return trip to the garage, I watched a delivery van pass in front of my house. Something niggled in my neck.

Madge wasn't home when I entered, so I showered, hoping she would make it when I finished. My cell phone lit when I picked it up from the counter. Madge texted she would be late again tonight because they couldn't find a doctor to replace the one that died. I sent back an okay because I had nothing to say. We were at an impasse. We were roommates, not spouses.

After watching a baseball game, I went to bed, waiting for the doorknob to rattle. When I hadn't heard it by 1:00 am, I gave into sleep. I heard nothing until my alarm blared me awake. Madge nestled in the blankets as she was sound asleep. Slipping out of bed and into the bathroom, I dressed in record time. Today was a big day for us, and I wanted to be ready.

On my walk into the office from the lot, I stopped by the food kiosk that sat at the front door. The operator was a big guy, and he and I are somewhat friends. So every once in a while, I make a point to stop by and purchase something from him. Today it would be coffee and a banana, even though I wanted the gigantic blueberry muffin sitting on the case. The big guy snickered when I turned away.

Greta was true to her word. Five boxes sat at my desk when I walked through the door. The anticipation was too much. Jo was eager too because she ran into my back. After all, I blocked the doorway, staring at the boxes.

"What are you doing, Ryker? You're blocking the doorway." Jo quipped.

"I'm staring at the mound of work ahead of us. Five boxes. Somehow, I didn't picture so many. I thought maybe one box per murder." I explained as I walked to my desk.

Jo sidestepped around me and placed her items on her desk. She glanced at the boxes, then up at me. "The oldest murder is 2011. So, this is ten years old. That's a long time for a killer to go undetected."

I plucked a box from the stack and opened it, signing the tag to prove I did it. This box held the evidence from a murder in 2015. Someone found two people in their home stabbed to death. The case matches the Rivera's except for the killing method. Pictures came out of the box, then I sat in my chair while I studied them. The stabbing took place in their bedroom. Both lay in the bed, but the wife's body was upside down in bed. Her position suggests she tried to stop the killer, but he got to her first.

The bed is a bloody mess, apparently from the altercation with the lady. However, the man appears to be sleeping with no visible blood except at the wound. Then the further I went into the stack of pictures, I found what I needed. The killer stabbed the man in his heart. That renders a person useless to fight and to live.

I separated the photos into stacks. One for him, then one for her. Hers was next. She fought the killer but lost. Stab wounds riddled her body, with the deadly incision being the neck. The pictures show the lady with a gaping cut across her jugular. She bled out in the bed. The lady made the attacker angry.

Standing, I pilfered in the box, looking at the collected evidence. The bloody bedsheets lay folded inside a plastic bag. The prior detectives also secured footwear and the victims' bedclothes. I hoped there was another box associated with this murder because there wasn't much in front of me.

The victims' faces stared back at me. They were eerily similar to the Rivera's, not community-wise, just in their looks. The victims were married for ten years and without children. Their home sat south of Fort Worth in the lake area, and it appeared to be in a medium-income neighborhood, not as nice as the Rivera's. It also had a sticker in the front window and one in the back. The man sold fishing boats at a marina while the woman worked in the marina's office. A co-worker found them.

Jo mumbled to herself, just as I did, while we decided who and how the killer crossed paths with our victims. Without an answer to our questions, we began cataloging the information from the boxes. The first unsolved case was from November 2011. Someone brutally stabbed a female college senior while she lived in a downtown Ft. Worth condo. This scene was messy. The photos show blood spatter in the kitchen and dining area while the body laid across the family room floor. This victim died fighting for her life while no one heard the commotion. The time of death was between 1:00 am, and 3:00 am.

Once we sifted through the box, we realized there wasn't much evidence available. The scene provided tons of blood samples, but they matched the victims. A fiber lodged in a sofa pillow didn't yield results, and the doors showed no forced entry. I stated the obvious, "there isn't much to help us. It reminds me of the Rivera's evidence."

"You're right. That's the killer's MO. He enters his victim's home, murders them in the overnight hours, and leaves no trace of his visit." Jo stated as she studied the victim's photo. "She was pretty and younger than the Rivera's. Do serial killers change their victim appetite and killing methods? If so, this makes this killer even more ruthless. We would have no way to warn his next victim because it could be anybody."

"He's human. He'll make a mistake. They always do. If he's been killing since 2011, there's been advancements in technology since he began. We'll find him." I predicted, but I didn't suggest a timetable. Jo's right. This could take years.

We stood and walked to the break room. With one box complete, we needed a break. I poured coffee into the two white cups perched on the counter. One cup sported hot pink lipstick on the side. I grinned. Jo loves her colorful lipstick, but she favors hot pink.

Greta entered the room, heading for the coffee pot. As soon she stood beside me, she looked up. "Are you still growing, Ryker? I'd swear you are taller today." Then she laughed.

"Nope. Still right at 6'4". I hope I'm not growing. Maybe it's you. Are you wearing your high heels?" I countered.

"That's it. I left those at home for these comfy wedges. Now, I know why I wear heels. I feel short next to you." Greta patted me on the back and left.

Jo and I took a leisurely stroll around the office. Anything to keep us away from our desks for a minute.
Jo glanced at me, "are we tackling another box before lunch?"

"We'll start it, but we won't finish before lunch. I'm already hungry." Then, with my head tilted, I winked at Jo. She snickered.

The following two boxes contained the murder investigation of a couple who suffered fatal stabbings in their bed. They lived outside of Ft. Worth, but we handled the investigation. This case was four years later than the first. Wonder what caused him to take four years off? Or did he? We have the possibility of cold case murders in other areas of Texas. I blurted it out before I thought it through. "What are the odds our killer works in Texas, not just around Ft. Worth?"

"You're serious, aren't you? I hoped that was a question you just threw out to get my reaction, but you think it's possible. That's crazy, Ryker." Jo's head swung from left to right as she considered my question. "But it makes more sense than the killer skipping four years." Jo leaned back in her chair while rubbing her neck, then her fingers moved to her earring.

After I made the revelation, Jo proposed, "can we go to lunch? I need to think."

Without an answer, I stood. With a light breakfast, my hunger pains started long ago. "Where to?"

"I don't know. Pick something." Jo never glanced my way. This case has her twisted. So, I'll take her to her favorite restaurant.

We climbed into my thousand-degree car and instantly regretted the lunch idea. "How much hotter can it get?" I asked, not really looking for an answer as I reached for the air conditioning buttons. I flipped them on high, but hot air blew first, then we felt a slight measure of relief.

When I pulled into the Mexican restaurant parking lot, Jo looked at it, then stammered, "can we eat inside?" Then she laughed as I wiped the sweat from my upper lip.

Lunch was nice and comfortable. We chatted about the case. Jo hinted at my marriage, but I didn't elaborate. Now wasn't the time to discuss it because I needed to talk to Madge first. Then, I'd share with Jo. She understood but wanted more, or her eyes said she wanted more. Those eyes get to me.

Our return to the office was quiet. We listened as our dispatchers sent our uniform officers all over the city. They answered many calls, including traffic accidents, burglary, and robbery calls, and silent alarms. Those were the worst because you never knew what you would face.

Our boxes sat on our desks just as we left them. So, we picked up right where we left off. The afternoon ended after box three. We learned nothing new from boxes two and three. Both murders were similar in design as they had very little evidence, no DNA from anyone other than the victim, and no forced entry. While the first case was messy, this one wasn't as much. Since I reviewed this case earlier, I summarized it for Jo.

Holding the Rivera's photo, Jo placed it alongside a picture of these victims. Again, strange similarities jumped from the glossy photo paper. "Isn't this odd? But the first murder was an unmarried college-aged female. Could this be the same killer?"

I stared at the photos, too. "Anything is possible." I plucked my phone from my desk. "With it being late in the day, how do you feel about saving the last two boxes for the morning? Once we review those, we can draft our report to Greta."

"Sounds like a plan." Jo reached under her desk and pulled her gym bag from underneath. "See you in the morning, Ryker." I watched Jo trot to the ladies' room to change clothes.

As I stood at my desk, I considered texting Madge. Instead, I went to the gym. I needed to work off growing frustration. Between my personal life and now this case, my body gave me signs of stress. This decision was the best I'd made in a while. I felt like a new person when I headed home.

On my drive home, my phone rang. I dug it out of my shorts pocket. The number was unfamiliar, but I answered anyway. It was Madge's hospital, but she wasn't calling. Instead, a nurse told me Jo asked her to call because she was in an accident. I don't remember telling the nurse goodbye. Instead, I dropped my phone in the cupholder, flipped the sirens on, and headed for the hospital.

I jogged into the emergency waiting room. There was a nurse on the phone, and she held her index finger in the air, telling me to be patient. I wasn't a patient person, but I tried. Then I rehashed my original conversation, and the nurse referenced Jo.

She stated Jo asked her to call me, so that means she is awake and talking. I took several deep breaths.

The nurse behind the desk dropped the phone in her pocket, looked at me, and asked, "Detective Bartley?"

"Yes." I showed her my badge. She grinned and walked around the desk.

"Let me lead you to Detective Samples." I followed her through the locked door. We passed several rooms before she turned right into a corner room. I followed her through the door and saw Jo lying on a hospital bed. My heart fell into my stomach. I'd never witnessed Jo sick, much less in a hospital.

Jo opened her eyes when she heard us enter. "Ryker, thanks for coming. I didn't know who else to call."

"I'm glad you thought of me. What happened, Jo? When I saw you last, you were going for a run." I stood beside the bed, holding her hand. The doctors bandaged her other hand and her forearm.

"Last I remember, I was running on the sidewalk heading back to the office. Then a man woke me as they loaded me onto a stretcher. The EMT said a car struck me as I crossed a street, but the car left the scene. A passerby saw the accident and called for an ambulance. The police took their statement. I haven't spoken to anyone yet." Jo inspected her hand injury, then she looked at me.

"We'll find out who did it. What are your injuries?" It worried me more than I wanted to admit seeing Jo in a hospital bed.

"So far, all I know is a cut hand and a scraped forearm, a bruised head, hip, and elbow from my landing. If this all there is, I'll call it lucky." Jo said as she sipped water from a Styrofoam cup. We listened as someone spoke outside her room, then we heard a soft knock.

.

Chapter 4

Officer Hutton grinned at me when I opened Jo's door. "Hutton, are you here for Jo's statement?"

"Yes, Detective. Greta asked me to handle the case." He entered as he shook my hand. Hutton walked over to Jo's bed and told her how sorry he was for her pain.

Jo and Hutton spoke for a few minutes, but with Jo's back to the vehicle, she saw nothing. No one screamed at her to get out of the way. The impact happened so fast, there was no time to react. Hutton explained he's pulling CCTV videos of cars in the area. The witness accounts were helpful, and he is confident they will find the culprit.

I stepped outside with Hutton after his conversation with Jo. "Thanks, Hutton, for handling this. I know you had a choice since you're recovering too."

"When I heard it was Jo, there was no way I'd turn it down. I've got it handled. Take care of her, Bartley. She's good for you." Hutton winked at me then left. I stared at his back while his last statement puzzled me. Wonder why Hutton told me Jo is good for me?

Jo tried to sit up in the bed but groaned, and I heard her as I entered. "Where are you going? The doctor hasn't released you yet. Lay back and relax." I pulled my chair closer to her bed and sat. When she realized I wasn't leaving, she laid her head back on the pillow and closed her eyes.

Ninety minutes passed before we saw the doctor again. He tapped on the door before entering. "Good news. Your x-rays are clean, but you have several areas of bone bruising, especially your elbow and hip. Those are painful, so prepare yourself. You must change the bandages on your hand and arm daily to prevent infection, and I'm prescribing fourteen days of antibiotics for that. I'm asking you to rest for forty-eight hours, but I know you probably won't. So, Detective Bartley, it's up to you to monitor her. If she slurs her words or can't focus, she needs to see a doctor asap. With that, I'll process the discharge papers." We had no questions since the rules were simple. However, Jo isn't one to follow the rules when it's her health. I've never known her to take a sick day.

A nurse rolled a wheelchair into Jo's room, and Jo wanted to turn the nurse and the chair away, but my eyes told her to keep quiet. So, she gingerly slid from the bed to the wheelchair, never looking at me. I pulled the car up to the door and helped Jo into the vehicle. She laid her head back, then stated, "take me to the station to get my car, please."

"Why can't I take you home? We can get your car tomorrow." I balked.

"Because I don't like being at home without a car. Please, Ryker. You've done enough for me for one night." Instead of commenting, I drove to the office. Jo asked me not to help, so I didn't. Her face showed a myriad of emotions. Mostly anger for her current situation.

Without telling Jo, I followed her home. I wanted her inside with the door locked before I left to go home. I checked my phone since it was after midnight, and there were no messages from Madge. This time, it didn't shock me. Nor did I worry. I had something to fill the void.

Jo stood outside her car, chuckling, when I climbed from my car. "Why doesn't this shock me, Ryker?"

"I needed to make sure you were home and locked inside before I left you alone." I followed Jo into the house. It had been a while since I was inside. "Can I get you anything to eat or drink?"

Jo shook her head as she stared at me. The silence left me nervous. We've never been in this situation before. Jo's eyes moved first. Then, she looked at her bandaged hand. The blood spot grew in size from her driving effort.

"Do you want me to stay tonight? I'm supposed to make sure you're okay." I asked, but it sounded awkward.

Jo's eyes did that thing again, then she answered, "yes, I'd enjoy the company, but not until you settle things with Madge." Now that she said it out loud, I didn't know what to think. I stepped closer to her but refrained from taking her in my arms.

"Let's get a new bandage for your hand, then I'll leave." She passed by me close enough for our arms to brush against the other. I sighed.

Jo had a stash of medical supplies, just like the rest of us cops. We never know what to expect when we go to work. I gently removed the bandage, and the cut was more profound than I expected. While I held it over the sink, I treated it with antiseptic, applied butterfly strips, and covered it with more gauze. Then I walked Jo to her bedroom and instructed her to rest. I didn't dare enter the room out of fear.

I turned my back on Jo and let myself out the door with the full intention of going home to sleep. But, instead, when I walked into my empty house, I showered, changed clothes, and returned to Jo's. I felt guilty leaving Jo, anyway. So I texted Jo I'd see her in a bit and not shoot me as an intruder. She returned a red heart.

Staring at the red heart, my emotions bubbled. Madge had never sent me a red heart, nor have I sent her one. Does that mean anything?

Jo unlocked the door before I made it back. She stood in the kitchen drinking a glass of milk. Her face was pale, but her eyes were bright. Maybe the pain caused her color to fade.

"Are you okay? You should be resting." I asked to break the tension between us.

"I was resting until I had to unlock the door. So why are you here, Ryker?" Jo's eyes bore a hole straight through me.

Why was I here in Jo's kitchen? Guilt, loneliness? "I felt guilty leaving you alone. I gave the doctor my word I'd watch you. So, here I am." Jo read straight through my explanation, but she didn't question it.

She returned to her room while I camped out on the sofa. I couldn't stretch out because the couch was too short, so I hung my feet over the arm. I listened as Jo paced around her room. Is my presence keeping her awake, or are her injuries too painful to sleep?

The next thing I knew was the coffee aroma floating in front of my nose. When I raised from the sofa, Jo leaned against the counter, staring in my direction. I ran my hand through my hair before I stood. "How do you feel this morning?"

"Like a freight train made several passes across my body. But I'm still going to work. So please don't try to stop me. My head is fine, and my body is sore." Jo explained.

"Can I talk you into staying here until lunch? That would give you a few more hours to rest." Her head swung from left to right before I finished my sentence. "If you refuse to stay here, then I'm driving you to the office." I held my hand in the air stopping the retort.

I sipped coffee after getting ready for work, waiting by the kitchen counter, then I inspected the condo while I had the time. Jo kept a tidy home. Her brown leather furniture was worn but comfortable. There was a flat-screen TV sitting atop a table facing the sofa. Then, Jo came out of her room, mumbling, but I didn't question her need to work. That's something we have in common, our love of the job.

We walked to my car in silence. I opened Jo's door for her and stood back as she sat on a bruised hip. She grimaces but doesn't complain. Jo glances at me, "thanks, Ryker. It was nice knowing someone had my back last night." Then she turned her head to face the road.

"I'll always have your back. Never forget that." I emphasized my feelings probably more than I should have. But then, I felt awful for not checking on Madge, but she didn't check on me either. Were we playing a game? Who contacts the other one first? I don't know what we're playing, but I don't like it.

Jo entered the detective's division before me. The other members heard about her incident and wanted to listen to her side of the story. First, she described what she remembered then they asked about her injuries. During her show and tell with the hand and arm, Greta called for Jo. Jo gave me a quick glance, then wandered off to meet Greta in her office.

While Greta and Jo spoke, I unpacked the last two boxes. Once we finished these, Greta wanted our decision on the murderer. Do we think the same killer is responsible for all the murders? My decision remains 50/50.

In July 2018, a man took a bullet to the head while standing in his kitchen. The detectives believed the killer and the victim surprised each other. The victim didn't expect the killer, and the killer didn't expect the victim to be in the kitchen. When the killer pulled the trigger, the victim dropped his drinking glass to the counter first, then his falling momentum carried some of the broken glass to the floor. The bullet struck the man in the head, and upon exit, it tore a swath into a kitchen cabinet. The killer took the time to dig out his slug and retrieve his spent brass.

I heard Jo speak to another detective as she limped to her desk. "Ryker, Greta wants to see you." I stared at her but said nothing. What does Greta want? It's not time for our decision yet.

"Greta, Jo said you needed to see me." I poked my head in the door.

"Come on in, Bartley. I wanted to make sure you are okay with Jo working. She said you drove her today, and I appreciate that. She doesn't need to be here, but that's beside the point. Jo won't leave, so don't let her drive for a few days until she gets mobility back in that hip. Thanks for taking care of her last night." Greta's last statement had more sincerity in it than anything I've heard since I started working here.

"Absolutely, Greta. I wouldn't leave any of you stranded at a hospital. By the way, thanks for putting Hutton on the case." I grinned because it wasn't time to get into my emotional turmoil.

"I hope it didn't cause any issues with Madge." Greta's right eyebrow lifted as if she knew something I didn't.

"No, it didn't." I didn't elaborate on our lack of communication, hoping to end this conversation.

"I'll let you get back to it. Let me know when you have a decision on the murders." Greta smiled at me as I turned to leave. Does everyone know I have feelings for Jo, or do I imagine it?

While I was away, Jo perused the documents on the third murder. "Ryker, what did Greta want with you? Are you supposed to take me home now?" Jo asked with sarcasm.

"No, you're staying, but you can't drive for a few days until your hip is better. Then we have to watch the hand. Greta's concerned, that's all." After I lifted a stack of photos from my desk, I wished I hadn't. Brain matter stuck to kitchen cabinets in this man's house. The killer must have stood close to the victim to cause that much damage, and no one heard the shot. "What time did the medical examiner put on this death?"

"Somewhere between 2:00-4:00 am."

"That's why the neighbors heard nothing." I nodded in acknowledgment. We spent an hour discussing this case and measuring these attributes against the other murders. Once we compiled our notes, we sat back in our chairs, pondering the cases. Could the same killer have murdered all these people?

"Well, what are your thoughts, Jo? We need to let Greta know something today." I asked because I had my decision.

"Can we eat lunch before we see Greta?" Jo pleaded.

"Let's go." I stood at my desk as Jo lifted herself from her chair. She never groaned loud enough for anyone to hear but me. Jo is in pain, but she'd never say it to the group. I noticed blood seeped through the hand bandage. "We need a bandage change too, while we're out."

Jo nodded without words. We walked to the elevator and waited for our ride. Then Jo gasped.

"What's wrong?" My heart hammered in my chest.

"I left the bag with the bandages on my desk. Sorry, Ryker. I'll be back." Jo turned before I stopped her.

"I'll get it. You hold the door." I trotted to her desk and returned just as the doors slid open. "Perfect timing." I grinned as I motioned Jo inside the empty car.

Lunch was subdued, which isn't typical for us. We usually laugh and joke, but with Jo in pain, that wasn't possible. While we waited for our food, Madge gave in and texted me, checking in with me. I sent back working a serial killer case, and I'd be home some time tonight for clothes. Madge returned a text with an ok. Is this how marriage works? Something tells me not all marriages are like mine. I married her to have a companion, not a texting partner.

Jo watched me interact with Madge, but she never questioned me. When I received the last text, I slid the phone into my pocket. The meal came, and I dug in because I didn't want to talk marriage, and I was hungry. Jo ate most of her food, and for that, I was grateful. When something troubles Jo, she stops eating, and right now, she needs the calories for recovery.

Once lunch ended, we drove to the station, and while sitting in the car, I changed her bandages. I started with the elbow, and it was in much better condition than the hand. When I unwound the gauze covering the hand wound, I grimaced. It seems stitches would have helped the wound close, but the doctor didn't want to stitch it because of its location. The doctor explained since the gash ran from the palm of Jo's hand and passed through the thumb and index finger, it would be best for Jo if the incision closed itself. Wounds that heal from inside out have less chance of infection. I tried not to hurt her, but I imagine moving it hurt. She handed me the butterfly strips, which I applied, then I re-wrapped the wound.

We returned to our desks with a mission. First, I faced Jo, then I asked, "what's your take on these murders? Do you think the same killer murdered the Rivera's along with these unsolved cases?"

Jo paused before she answered. "I'm 90% sure the same killer committed these murders. We have no spent brass, no DNA at any scenes, no signs of forced entry, and all occurred during early morning hours. Our evidence points to the same person. I just wonder how many more murders are sitting unsolved in Texas with our same MO?"

Her comments brought a smile to my face. We always think alike. "You took the words right out of my mouth. Are you ready to meet with Greta and give her the news?"

Jo lifted her shoulders. "Might as well. She won't be happy, but I think she suspects it."

After grabbing our notes, I followed Jo into Greta's office. While Jo still moved slow, her color was better this afternoon, and her hand bandage wasn't red. So maybe that was a good sign too.

As we entered Greta's office, she stood at her window with her cell phone to her ear. When Jo spotted Greta, she stopped in mid-stride, and I almost knocked her over. I caught her with one hand and stood her up while I chuckled. We waved at Greta and motioned we would wait. Just as we stepped out of her office, she called us back.

"I hope you're here with your decision," Greta stated.

"We are," I replied as we sat across from her. "We are 90% sure we have a serial killer, but we think he might travel Texas, not just the Ft. Worth area." That stopped Greta in her tracks.

"Wow. That was a surprise. How did you come to that conclusion?" She inquired as she jotted notes.

We outlined each case, and in the end, Greta agreed. After that, ideas bounced across her desk about how to proceed. "Do you want to work the cases we have before asking other departments for their unsolved cases?"

Jo and I shared a glance. We hadn't thought about that yet. "Let's work these cases for a couple of days. We haven't had the chance to study the photos or read all the reports. Then, if we find nothing, we'll ask you to start the process." I looked at Jo for agreement. She gave it to me with a head nod.

As we stood to leave, Greta instructed, "take the small conference room for your command center. You'll have tons of paper and boxes if this thing grows."

Jo entered the small conference room and took a seat while I transported the case files from our desk to the new staging area. In my absence, Jo designed the room, and she instructed me where to place the boxes. I plopped into a chair once everything was to Jo's liking. Scanning the room, I understood the rationale behind her instructions as the room flowed from one case to the next in chronological order.

I stepped out of the office and returned, holding two steaming cups of coffee. Jo sighed. "How did you know I wanted this?" She questioned.

"I needed coffee, so I thought you might relish one too. Let's start at the 2011 murder of the college girl and work our way forward. We'll do this round together. Write anything you feel important." Jo gave me a slight nod as she sipped her coffee.

We each read the detective's transcript of the murder scene, the lab findings and potential witnesses and suspects. Our crime lab found one fiber that matched nothing in the condo. There were no witnesses, and no one heard anything coming from her condo the night of the murder. The victim's boyfriend provided an airtight alibi for the night of the murder. He was at his parent's house in Austin because his dad had surgery the day before. The murder shocked the boyfriend and the victim's best friend because everyone loved her. The police released her body to her parents two weeks after the murder for burial in a Ft. Worth cemetery. Her parents show a Ft. Worth address at the time of their daughter's death. Wonder if they're still there? Although, I don't want to drag them through the death investigation again.

Then, we moved to the crime scene pictures. The scene was messy, and that's where I scratched my head. Could this be the same killer? The Rivera's crime scene wasn't chaotic like this. If the killer began with this murder, was he learning his craft? The more I thumbed the pictures, the more I felt the victim heard the killer, and she approached him. They met in the hallway between the back door and her bedroom. I shared my thoughts with Jo.

"Your description makes sense with the blood spatter along the hallway walls. If the victim heard the killer, she would have fought for her life. That brings up another question if she fought the killer, why wasn't there skin or blood under her nails? From her photo, she had long nails."

"Were any of her nails broken?" I inquired further.

"From the picture angles, I saw none broken, but the little finger and ring finger on the left hand are out of sight. Find the autopsy report, and let's read it." Jo suggested while she flipped papers in the murder book.

She removed the report from the binder and glanced over it. Then she passed it to me. There was no mention of a broken nail or evidence under her nails. I understood why the case turned cold. No witnesses or suspects turn cases cold quickly.

Our afternoon flew by as we rehashed each case. The cases in order are 2011, 2015, 2018, then the Rivera's in 2021. Neither Jo nor I could find a correlation between the victims. All were mid to upper-class people who lived in nice homes with stable jobs, except for the college girl. She was a student with no work listed.

Jo looked up from the last stack of photos. "All the murders occurred during the same time in the overnight hours. Does our killer have a day job, then he kills at night?"

I nodded as I considered this information. A profile began forming in my mind, but I didn't share. We finished the other cases then took a break. We wanted to discuss our results before we left for the day.

Both of us agreed the killer changed his practices after the first murder in 2011 of the college girl. The other scenes weren't messy. If anything, the killer cleaned before he left. The first murder victim had a calendar, but the appointments were shorthand, never deciphered. The crime scene techs found no prints at the other scenes, leading us to believe the killer wore gloves during the crime. Also, the prior detectives never determined how the killer entered the homes.

We learned nothing new on the second pass through the files. There were unsolved murder cases with little to no clues or evidence. I leaned back and rubbed my neck. "I'm hungry. So, I'll drop you home, grab clothes and pizza and come back over, if that's okay."

Jo looked at me, and I wasn't prepared for what I saw. "Ryker, you don't have to babysit me anymore. I'm fine."

"I'm not babysitting. You need help to get around, and I want to be there." We stared at each other until Jo moved her eyes. I was proud of myself for holding out.

"Sounds good to me. I'll need to stop for more gauze because I'm almost out."

"I'll stop for it on my way to your house. Come on, let's get out of here. I'm too frustrated to think, anyway." I turned back, closed the office door, and followed Jo outside into the early evening heat. Heat radiated from the asphalt parking lot. I grimaced when I opened my car door. You couldn't breathe inside the car even with the air conditioning blowing on high. We were halfway to Jo's before we noticed a difference.

"Did the magnifying glass help with any of the photos? You're better at spotting the tiniest of details. I hope something would jump out at you." Jo chuckled when she saw my face.

I shook my head, "No, nothing jumped. The other cold cases I've worked on held more evidence than what we have. These crime scenes are too clean. The killer blatantly teases the police. He leaves the scene with so little evidence that I'm leaning toward an ex-law enforcement officer or someone with an interest in criminal justice. Your regular person wouldn't know how to keep their DNA from a murder scene."

"I wondered when the profiling would begin. I hear it has, and I agree so far." When I pulled into Jo's drive, I helped her climb from the car. Knowing she's inside made me feel better. Something shifted in me when I came close to losing Jo.

As I drove to my house, I profiled the killer in my head. I'm not ready to share with Greta, but I'll share the rest with Jo tomorrow. I should have a partial profile, anyway.

Once again, my house sat dark. I plucked the mail from our mailbox at the end of the drive. There was days' worth tucked inside. I couldn't tell if Madge were home. Everything looked the same as I tossed the mail on the counter on the way to our room.

I showered while I could, changed into jeans and a t-shirt, slid on boat shoes, grabbed tomorrow's clothes, and headed for the pharmacy for more gauze. Without knowing how long Jo would need to wrap her hand and elbow, I bought all they had. With luck, she would have some leftovers.

With the pharmacy bag, my duffel and the pizza box, my hands were full. I walked to the door, and before I knocked, Jo opened the door. She had changed too. Even without her flashy lipstick, she's drop-dead gorgeous. Her eyes roved over my chest as I passed her.

We chatted while we ate and laughed at a few of our childhood stories. Jo put on a movie, and we watched it until she fell asleep. When I turned off the television, she bolted awake. "Sorry, Ryker. See you in the morning. Thanks for staying again." Her fingers brushed my arm as she walked to her room. I laid my head on the sofa. What was I doing?

The following day I woke before my alarm. I slept better last night than the night before. The coffee sat ready before Jo appeared. She looked more rested today too. "Can we change the bandage here instead of the car?" She sipped her coffee and sighed.

"Here's your gauze." I placed the bag on the kitchen table. Jo laughed, then I said, "I was unsure how much you needed, so I bought it all." I lifted my shoulders.

"Thanks, Ryker. How much do I owe for all of this?" Jo looked at me. "I don't know what I would have done without you. It wouldn't have been easy."

"You owe me nothing. You'd do it for me." I wanted to hug her, but I didn't budge. Instead, I promised myself a talk with Madge by the weekend. "Let's get this bandage changed." While I worked on the bandage, I asked, "Are you ready for work?"

Jo nodded, and once I placed the last bit of tape, we headed for the door. We stepped outside to another scorching August day. Clouds sat at the horizon, taunting us. On our way to the office, Jo treated me to one of her special coffees and a muffin from heaven. I don't know what the bakers put in their muffins, but they are delicious. I've tasted nothing else that comes close to these muffins.

On our way upstairs to our office, Jo asks, "are you ready to share your profile? I know you have one."

Chapter 5

I didn't answer, but I grinned. She knows me too well. I've been working on a profile, and it's time to unveil it. "I'll share when we get situated because I'd rather discuss it with you before we meet with Greta."

Jo cocked her head at me, wondering why I took that stance. Usually, I spout out whatever comes to mind. But this killer is different. If what I think is true, stopping him will be a monumental task.

On the way to our desks, we passed a few co-workers heading to a crime scene. We spoke briefly and let them get on their way. Greta wasn't in her office yet, so it turned out to be perfect timing for us. As soon as Jo sat behind her desk, she stated. "I'm ready for the big reveal." She picked up her pen and slid a notebook in front of her. I chuckled because she always takes notes about everything.

"I based this profile on the information we have so far. Our killer is a male between 30-40 years old, divorced, controlling, above average intelligence, an avid planner, and he attempted a job in law enforcement."

I raised my eyes from my notes, and Jo stared at me.

"What? Why are you staring, Jo? Do you not agree?" I prodded.

"I absolutely agree. But I'm curious how you determined all of this with so little case information."

"Well, for starters, a man has more chance killing someone with a garotte than a woman because of strength. It takes a considerable amount of force to kill a person using a garrote. The other traits I determined from the crime scenes. Since the scenes are without DNA, that would make our killer intelligent, and he plans his kills, so he knows the best time to strike."

Jo smiled. "I need to take profiling lessons from you. You described the killer as having above average intelligence. However, I bet he doesn't know he has a brilliant detective on his heels. If anyone can identify the killer, it's you, and I'm along for the ride."

I shuffled papers on my desk because I wasn't sure what to do next. "Should we share the profile with Greta? I haven't seen her this morning yet."

"I didn't see her when we arrived. That's unusual. I'll step out and see if she's available." Jo walked through the doorway, and I took a deep breath. While I waited for Jo, I jotted the dates of death for our cases.

Two deaths occurred in July and one in November. Then next to the death dates, I listed the day of the week for the murder. November 24, 2011 was a Thursday. The subsequent murder happened on a Tuesday, followed by a Sunday murder. Thus, I spotted the pattern of deaths occurring in July and November on Tuesday, Thursday, and Sunday. Thanks to my being a savant, I can recall this information from my brain, no need for the internet.

My scribbled notes lay on the desk in front of me. What does this information tell me? Does it help move the case forward? It further proves we have a serial killer in our midst.

Jo entered and studied the notes. "Can you explain your scribbles while Greta is on the phone?"

I paused before I spoke. This information was new to me, too, and I wasn't sure about sharing it with Greta. But I shared it with Jo. As I recounted the information I discovered, her mouth hung open in astonishment. "Just to be clear, you found the pattern by accident, and you knew the weekday that corresponded to the date of deaths." Jo's eyebrow lifted, "I suppose that's part of your brain thing."

"Yeah, I guess it is. I didn't have it as a child. Only after my injury could I recite the weekday for any calendar date. When I put it on paper, the pattern was there." I explained.

"What pattern?" Greta inquired. Her face bestowed the seriousness of her question.

Jo explained what happened in her absence while Greta studied me. I sat still.

Greta asked me questions, which I answered. Then, she wanted the details on the pattern. Jo stood at the board, and as I rehashed the particulars, she transcribed them on our board. Greta stood and stared at the board for a full five minutes without speaking.

"Ryker, why would the killer commit murder only in July and November?" Greta questioned.

"I feel something happened personally to the killer during those months. It could have been a birth, a death, a marriage or a divorce. We won't have those answers until we capture him." I explained. Then I continued, "Everything a serial killer does is for a reason."

She agrees Ft. Worth, Texas, has a serial killer working their streets, but she must rule out other Texas areas. If the killer has free rein in Texas, the federal group might try to take over the case.

I shook my head no. I wanted to crack this case. "Greta, we found it. See if they'll give us time to crack it. If we can, it would be a mighty big feather in the Ft. Worth Police Departments' hat."

"I'll keep it as low-key as possible." Then Greta advised she has a contact in the Dallas Police Department, and she'll contact Detective Cabello before breaking the news to the captain. If it turns out the killer moves around Texas doing the same, we have a bigger problem, and she's required to notify the captain.

Greta stood and almost trotted out of our office. I shook my head as I considered giving this case away. "Jo, I don't want to give this case away."

"I know, Ryker. We'll keep it as long as we can. No one else spotted it but you. They should let you run with it." Jo declared. She reached up and swiped the eraser across the board. There was no sign of the dates and the weekdays. They would keep that information close. Only the profile details remained on the board.

With a phone to her ear, Greta reappeared in my office. She closed the door and asked us if we could meet Detective Cabello at 1:00 pm today. Jo and I shrugged our shoulders and agreed.

Greta relayed the information to the detective and then texted him the address. She turned to face us, "Detective Cabello and Detective Jones are bringing three cases with them. They have the same attributes as the Rivera's. Their cases are from 2014, 2015, and 2017. All three cases are unsolved with clean crime scenes, no DNA and no witnesses. He understands we aren't sharing our information yet. I trust him, so you should too. Grab lunch and be on time." Greta turns and leaves us standing in awe.

I sit and ponder our next meeting. We have four cases. Dallas has three, so how many more are there that we nothing about?

"Ryker, let's do as Greta suggests. I'm hungry, and I can't think when my stomach growls." Jo stood and grimaced.

"What's wrong, Jo?" I watched as pain rippled through her body. First, her face turned pale, then when the pain subsided, the color returned.

"I turned wrong, I guess. Sometimes I get these pains that race down my leg from my hip, and they take my breath away. Once it passes, I'm okay. But, come on, the pains don't slow my hunger." She grinned.

With not much time for lunch, we opt for a food truck hot dog. This guy has the best hot dogs of anyone in town. We try to eat with him once a week, but we might make it twice if our week is hectic. The hot dogs are massive, so it only takes one to satisfy anyone's hunger pains. Then if you pair it with his famous lemonade, it's the best lunch around. We enjoy our food under a red umbrella along the sidewalk. My only issue was the sweat running down my face. I didn't have enough napkins to keep up between the hot dog and the sweat, but it was worth it.

We ate in record time and was glad to be back indoors. I didn't want to meet Detective Cabello with a soaked shirt. By the time he and his partner arrived, we had cooled, and so had our clothes. At exactly 1:00 pm, Detectives Cabello and Jones greeted Greta with a handshake while Cabello threw in a peek on her cheek. I saved that tidbit for later.

Greta introduced us as our guests took seats around the conference table. Cabello removed the box top and placed it on the floor beside his chair. His first question caught me off guard.

"Detective Bartley, can you share your reasons for thinking we have a serial killer roaming Texas?"

Glancing at Greta, she nodded, so I proceeded. I shared everything but the dates of death and the corresponding weekday. Greta never mentioned it either. She knows I want to see their files first before sharing something of that magnitude.

My explanation satisfied Detective Cabello because he lifted three murder books from the box and placed them on the table. He began with the oldest murder, which occurred in a neighborhood northeast of Dallas in July 2014. Cabello described the scene. The killer suffocated the female victim with her bed pillow. There were no signs of forced entry, and nothing else appeared disturbed in the victim's home.

Second, this murder was in November 2015 in Dallas, where someone shot a man to death while he slept. It took one bullet to the right temple. The crime lab found no bullet casing at the scene. The medical examiner found the mangled slug embedded in the victim's skull, and the bullets condition took away any chance of using it as a comparison. Again, there were no signs of forced entry or other disturbance.

Jo and I exchanged a glance. These murders matched ours. Now, I wonder how long this has been happening? If we hadn't spotted it, he could have gone on forever, or until he tired of it.

Cabello rubbed the murder book, then stated, "this is our case. We worked every lead that came in, and despite that, we found nothing. This murder happened northwest of Dallas in July 2017. A man lying in bed took a bullet to the head. This time, the bullet entered between the eyes instead of the temple. The man's wife returned from a work trip on a Thursday and found him. The medical examiner confirmed he had been dead forty-eight to seventy-two hours when his wife found him."

Jo spoke first. "Wasn't the wife concerned when she didn't speak with her husband while she was away?"

"Her alibi was ironclad. She's in pharmaceutical sales, and she was attending a conference at some resort in Miami. The wife explained when she's away at a conference, there may be days when they didn't speak. Jones accounted for her time too. She gave us no enemies and no reason for someone to kill her husband. Without a witness, we had zip." Cabello explained.

I nodded because I agreed. When the leads dry up, there is nowhere else to go with an investigation. "There is one other piece of the puzzle I'd like to share." I stood and placed myself in front of the whiteboard.

With the list of murders in my hand, I notated each date of death followed by the corresponding weekday. The list was seven murders long. Cabello and Jones leaned back in their chairs as they pondered the new information. Jones let out a whistle while Cabello rubbed his neck.

Cabello turned to face Greta. "Did you know about this?"

"Yes, I did. Ryker discovered it earlier. We're not sharing with anyone yet, especially the public. We want to keep the killer in the dark for as long as possible, and we'd appreciate you keeping it under wraps, too, just for the time being."

"We'll keep it quiet as long as we can." Cabello offered while Jones nodded his agreement.

The Dallas Detectives packed their boxes. As they left, they advised they would revisit their cases and be in touch with us. We stayed rooted to our chairs because we'd proven Texas has unsolved murders in Dallas and Ft. Worth with the same attributes. There's not a person around that wouldn't believe it's the same killer.

Greta cut us loose for the rest of the day. Now, we plan the next steps. Do we alert Texas to a potential serial killer, or do we hold off for a bit?

As I drove Jo home, we discussed the case. Jo wants to discuss with other departments while I want to keep it to ourselves for a while longer. I realize we need to alert the other departments because the odds are this killer has been active for years. Cabello and Jones are reopening their cases. Maybe they will find something to lead us to the killer.

I followed Jo inside so I could change her bandage. She could probably handle it on her own now, but I wasn't ready to relinquish my duties. When the dressing fell away, I stated, "your hand looks good with only one place still open. The doctor will be pleased." I placed the new bandage in place and wrapped it. Then I looked into her eyes, and that was the wrong move. They did that thing again. I had to leave.

"I'm going to the gym. If you need anything, text me. I'll be by in the morning to get you." I backed away from Jo so temptation wouldn't win.

"Ryker, I can drive myself now. You said the gash was almost closed."

"That's my point. Almost closed isn't closed. I'll see you in the morning, and I'll text before I come." Grinning as I closed the front door and trotted to my car.

The gym was packed by the time I arrived. Changing clothes quickly, I jumped onto the last remaining treadmill. After a three-mile run, I moved to the weights, and from there, I spent time with a rowing machine. Finally, I stood from the device, glancing around the gym. Nervous energy still coursed through my body, but I called it quits. It was time to see if Madge made it home.

I grabbed my work clothes from the locker room and trotted to my car, hopeful Madge and I can start our discussion. I can't be the only one that feels lost. She's said nothing about her feelings, but that doesn't mean she isn't questioning our marriage.

Pulling into the driveway, I raised the garage door, and my heart sunk again. Madge wasn't home. This time I sent a text. Seconds later, Madge responds, stating she'll be home in two hours. I showered, dressed in casual clothes, and found something to eat. At the two-hour mark, I got mad when Madge didn't show as promised.

At the three-hour mark, I texted Madge I would be at work. She replied with a measly okay. No explanation and she didn't ask for forgiveness for standing me up again.

Instead of work, I stood outside of Jo's door in the dead of night, wondering if I should do this or not. Before I got my answer, she opened the door.

"Ryker, what are you doing here?" Jo leaned against the door waiting for me to explain. I wasn't sure I could, so I shrugged my shoulders.

Jo stepped aside for me to enter. I walked into the kitchen in search of coffee. Jo offered, "I'm watching a movie if you're interested. Popcorn is on the table."

"That sounds nice. I'll join you." I answered, but I never looked at her.

"How's Madge, Ryker? Something is up, or you wouldn't be here night after night." Jo knew when trouble hit me, and this time was no different.

Over the next thirty minutes, I spilled my guts to my work partner. Something I said I'd never do. Work is work until it isn't. Jo's eyebrows lifted when I confessed Madge and I were moving in opposite directions. Jo didn't offer to solve our problem, but she made a superb listener.

Then she stated, "I'll be here when you're ready, Ryker. If not, we're still working partners, and I'm not giving that up." Jo reached over and hugged me.

The best hug I've had in months. I wanted to stay that way all night.

Jo started the movie again once my confessions were in the open. We ate popcorn and finished the movie. It turned out to be the most enjoyable of nights. Jo is healing, and I feel relieved for sharing my home life issues.

The following week nothing transpired on the serial killer cases. We spoke with Detectives Cabello and Jones, as they are reviewing their cases too. So far, they had nothing new.

I tried to get Madge to meet me at home again but to no avail. It makes me wonder if she would even speak to me if I handed her divorce papers. Her only concern is the hospital, and I can't compete with that.

Detective Cabello called the following day. They found a fiber from the 2015 crime scene, but they've not been able to match it. I asked him to forward me the crime lab stats on the fiber, and I would compare it to our fiber from 2018. We might get a match. He would secure the info from the lab and forward it, but it might be Tuesday since this is Labor Day weekend.

When Cabello reminded me of the long weekend, I texted Madge. The last I remembered, she's off work this weekend, but I know things change. She agreed to be home on Saturday morning for us to discuss our current arrangement. So, I finished my day and dropped Jo at her house after she promised to change her bandage.

With tonight being Friday, I didn't expect Madge home before midnight. That gave me time to get the place clean. Then, with luck, we could work on ourselves for the next two days. I had no intentions of letting my marriage fall apart without a fight, but if the other side doesn't feel the same, why try?

The house smelled musty when I entered. I guess when you leave it unattended for days, that's what you get. After I showered and dressed, I started on the house. First, the downstairs with the dusting and the vacuum. Then I sprayed something I found in the cabinet. Whatever it was, it sent me into a coughing fit. After a few minutes, the coughing subsided enough for me to continue with the upstairs chores.

I hadn't paid attention to the laundry basket in recent days. A strange sensation worked its way into my soul when I realized the basket only held my clothes. Where are Madge's work clothes? I've never seen the basket like this, and I was unsure how to feel about it.

By nine, I had eaten a bite and settled in front of the television. I knew I had several hours before Madge would arrive, so I dosed. Dreams had me in turmoil as I saw Jo lying in a hospital bed, then Madge stood off to the side laughing at me. Finally, at

11:45, I awoke with a start when the doorknob rattled.

Madge walked into the house carrying bags of dirty clothes. I chastised myself for my earlier thoughts. Then, walking over to her, I took the bags from her hands. We greeted one another without touching. I carried the bags upstairs to the laundry room while Madge followed. "Ryker, I'm taking a shower."

I nodded but said nothing. My thoughts were on my dream and the mound of dirty clothes at my feet. With so many pieces, I could only get a third into the washer. I didn't start it for fear I'd take Madge's hot water.

She reappeared shortly and laid beside me on the bed. "Can we start our talk in the morning? I'm sleepy."

"Of course, we can," I replied, trying to keep my tone neutral, even though I didn't feel it. I wanted this talk to happen now because I didn't know how long I could live with our so-called arrangement. We are either friends or spouses, and I needed to know which one.

We climbed into bed, and I fell into a dream-filled sleep, just like earlier. Serial killers, Jo, and Madge, all had a part in my dreams. When morning came, I awoke first and padded to the kitchen for coffee. Madge walked downstairs an hour later.

Madge suggested we sit at the table and start our conversation over coffee. So, we did. Madge started by accepting responsibility for our marriage failure. Her hospital hours are long, and there's no end in sight. I took responsibility, too, because my hours weren't the easiest either. We held hands sitting at the table, and we agreed to make it work, but that would take communication.

With the holiday weekend upon us, we hoped for downtime. I wasn't due until Tuesday unless something happened that required my presence, and the same went for Madge. So, over the next two days, we discussed our marriage and dreams for the future. It relieved us to know we both want the same thing in life.

Just as Madge's phone sounded in the early morning hours of Labor Day, mine followed. We stared at each other, not knowing how to act. Then, reaching our nightstands, we answered our phones. Madge responded to the hospital to help with overcrowding while I spoke to Greta about a triple shooting.

We backed out of the drive-in tandem. Madge went right while I turned left. Jo called wanting my status. She drove herself to the office against my wishes. But she said she needed to try it. Traffic was light at this early hour. Greta met Jo and me in her office with the preliminaries.

Greta admits to not having enough detectives for weekends like this. The scorching weather brings out the worst in people. Domestics top our call logs when the outside heat rises, and people are off work. So, here we are, working another holiday because people can't get along. Some things never change.

Greta assigned us to a triple shooting. Two participants are deceased, with one survivor at the hospital. The patrol officers mentioned the survivor is a known gang member. "We would like to stop anything else they have in mind. Can you two go to the hospital and see if the survivor is awake? Maybe he feels up to identifying his assailant?"

We grabbed our things from our desk and trotted to the car. "How did the hand feel driving?" I asked.

"I didn't use it. Over the weekend, I cleaned house, and I must have stretched it too far." Jo lifted her hand to my face, and the red blotch glowed in the dark.

"Jo, why didn't you let me drive you this morning? You shouldn't even be here. If that gash opens any further, you'll be in surgery." It frustrated me that Jo wouldn't call me, but I understood why. We have unspoken words between us.

She stared out the front window instead of answering. Neither of us spoke until we arrived at the hospital. We trotted into a full emergency room waiting area. As I glanced around, I understood why they called for Madge. This was a madhouse. I heard my name called, and I turned to find a patrol officer standing beside the admittance door.

"Daniels. Looks like Ft. Worth has been busy." I joked.

"Too busy, Bartley. Hi Samples. Looks like the hand is still giving you trouble."

Jo grinned, "apparently, I did too much housework. So what do we have, Daniels?"

Officer Daniels gave us the rundown. There was a triple shooting on the south side of town overnight involving rival gangs. Two gang members died from their injuries, with one survivor. He's waiting for surgery to remove a bullet.

I wasn't willing to wait for a nurse, so I let us into the emergency room area. Madge stood at the nurse's station. "Fancy meeting you here, Detective," Madge said with a slight grin.

"Did you have a shooting victim in here?" I asked in my professional voice.

Madge answered, "yes. He's in that room." She pointed to a room at the opposite corner. I waved and started that way. She tried to stop me, but it didn't work.

I walked into the victim's room and caught him watching television and dosing. He didn't appear to be in as much distress as they led me to believe. So why would Madge try to keep me from interviewing a victim?

Entering first, I flashed my badge. Jo did the same when she entered. Officer Daniels trailed us. After I identified myself and my partners, I asked him about the shooting.

The victim cleared his throat, and then he described the shooting, including the car and the shooter. He can't believe the other two guys are dead. The victim offered no name for the shooter. Instead, at the end of his story, he vowed retaliation.

Jo and I tried to persuade him to leave the gangs alone, but he shook his head as if he heard nothing we said. So, since there was nothing else to gain from this victim, we left him to his injuries.

I turned right from the lot heading back to the station. A half-block away from the hospital, Jo points to a car traveling in the opposite direction. "That's it, Ryker. The shooter's car just passed us."

"Hold on. I hope they aren't going to the emergency room to finish the job. With the number of people in the waiting room, that could be a bloodbath." Once I made a U-turn, I punched the pedal to the floor. We found the shooter's car parked at the outpatient door. I threw the car in the park, and we ran into the hospital. Just as we crossed the threshold, gunfire erupted.

People screamed as they ran from the emergency room as hospital workers scrambled to seek cover. Then, over the loudspeaker, someone called a code silver. That alerted the hospital staff to an active shooter situation, and they knew this wasn't a drill.

"Jo, call for back up. I'll search for the shooter. Keep your radio on." I sprinted through the emergency room area because I knew what I would find. As I suspected, nurses and doctors worked to save the victim, but their efforts were futile. The shooting victim died within minutes of taking his second gunshot of the night.

With my radio in one hand, I notified Jo that the victim died. Then Jo told me Officer Daniels reported hospital guards chased the shooter to the stairwell. The shooter was last spotted on the third floor, looking into rooms as we ran down the hallway.

Why is he doing that? Is a friend or relative a patient here?

Instead of running to the third floor, I listened to Jo. She asked me to return to her location. When I rounded the corner, she grinned because she wondered if I would listen. I've run headfirst into danger before.

"SWAT Commander Marsh would like a word." Jo pointed outside to the command unit sitting in the parking lot.

Chapter 6

"Let's go." We knocked on the door and waited for the entrance. Marsh opened the door for us, and we stepped into an air-conditioned vehicle.

"Bartley, Samples. Tell me what's happening in there. Our Team is on standby." Marsh barked.

I explained the situation starting from the first shooting and ending with the dead victim in the emergency room. The victim never made it to surgery. We have officers stationed at both emergency room doors, interior and exterior. The hospital is on lockdown, and they activated a code silver.

Commander Marsh speaks with his Team as they prepare for entry. Two teams of ten flank the emergency room doors. The first ten enter then spread out, searching for the assailant. They declare the emergency room cleared with all rooms inspected, and no one can exit or enter without police clearance.

The second set of SWAT members splits with one team taking the stairs on the right and the others taking a left. Commander Marsh kept Jo and me on the sidelines until they cleared the rest of the first floor. I mentioned the guards seeing the assailant on the third floor. So, we sat and listened to the communication between the teams.

SWAT cleared each floor, then stationed an officer at the exits to prevent the shooter's re-entry. Sitting by as others did their job was hard for me. I'm all about action, not sitting back. While one team worked on the third floor, my cell phone rang.

I stepped outside to answer as Madge told me she had a missing nurse. She described the nurse, and her service area is floors four through six. With this information, I entered the command unit and spoke to Commander Marsh. He relayed my information to his team. Then, he released Jo and me to help locate the nurse.

We entered the hospital at a full trot, never stopping for the police officer guarding the door. I wanted to start on floor four, so I took the stairs with Jo following. When we made it to the door, I peered through the door window glass to make sure I wasn't walking into an ambush. But, as far as I could tell, the coast was clear.

After slipping through the door, we plastered ourselves against the wall and crept toward the nurse's station. We almost made it when a SWAT Team walked toward us from the opposite side. They cleared floor four without so much as a visual of the shooter.

"Two floors to go. Take one room at a time." The SWAT leader barked.

We followed the team. The shooter is in this hospital somewhere. Where is he hiding? In our ear comms, we listened as the second SWAT Team cleared floor five. One floor remained, and it was ours.

The Team entered floor six with their weapons at eye level. Room by room, a team member searched the room, closets and bathrooms to no avail. One member reached for a doorknob when a sob sounded from inside. Two members stood on each side of the door with one guy positioned in front, and his gun faced the door.

On the count of three, the door flew open, and sitting on the floor, bound and gagged, was our missing nurse. Jo approached her and removed the bindings. The nurse described our shooter, but our hearts sunk when she told us he asked for scrubs. So now, we had a missing shooter wearing scrubs.
I relayed our latest intel to Commander Marsh when I heard Greta's voice. "Greta, we're fine. Jo is with me. Our hospital search is nearly complete."

We gathered outside the closet, where we found the nurse. The shooter was here somewhere, but where? Did he escape wearing the scrubs?

There weren't many patient rooms on the sixth floor, but I didn't realize how many surgical rooms this hospital had. One by one, we cleared them as most were in the dark. Finally, lights shone from one of the surgery rooms, but we heard no activity. I stopped the team's progression until we had surgery confirmation. We didn't need to barge into a surgical procedure and compromise the patient.

Madge confirmed there were no surgery procedures scheduled for the sixth floor. We found him. Our only issue was taking him alive without gunfire. A SWAT leader notified Commander's Marsh and Huxley of our impending entry.

We entered the room with guns drawn, following two SWAT members holding an active shooter response shield in front of their bodies. Once we crossed the threshold, we froze. The shooter sat curled in a corner with a gun to his head. Jo holds out her hand to stop me.

Jo speaks to the shooter. He doesn't move or speak. Jo walks closer, and I cringe. It's hard to see someone you care for put themselves in danger. Then, at four feet away, the guy spoke and said the victim in the emergency room shot and killed his sister. Jo spoke softly, trying to get the guy to hand over his gun.

The shooter stood and faced Jo. Then he raised his weapon and pointed it at her. We froze. Jo paled. But a SWAT member didn't wait. Instead, he shot the guy in the chest. The shooter crumpled to the floor. I raced to him, but I could do nothing to save him. He needed a doctor.

I called for Madge. She appeared with a team of nurses. Madge ushered us out of the room. We obliged. I radio the incident to Greta, and she's on her way to the sixth floor. Commander Marsh is following.

We camped out in the surgical waiting room while Madge works wonders with the shooter. The SWAT member's shot was clean as another person was in danger. No one will fault him for what he did today. He likely saved Jo's life. And for that, I was grateful.

Commander Marsh agrees it was a justified shooting, and the report will reflect the same. They lifted the hospital lockdown after three grueling hours. Commander Marsh and his SWAT team vacate the hospital now that the threat is over, leaving me with Greta and Jo. I wanted to be alone with Jo, but I couldn't fathom why. Greta talked, and I vaguely listened.

While we were together, we discussed the serial killer cases too. We mentioned asking another department, but we never agreed on it as Madge entered the waiting room. "I wondered if you'd still be here. The shooter survived the surgery, but I'm unsure if he'll live through the night. There were lots of organ damage. I repaired what I could." Madge lifted her hand in a half-hearted wave, turned, and walked out. She never came to me or asked me to step outside of the room. She simply stated her business at left.

When I realized what happened, Greta and Jo stared at me. Then I remember we need the shooter's identification. So I jumped up and ran to stop Madge. "Madge, we need the patient's identification. We're working to stop a gang war in the city."

"I'll send a nurse to the waiting room with it. I've not seen it."

"Ok. Thanks." I didn't know what else to say. So, I returned to the waiting room. I explained my abrupt departure.

"Good idea, Ryker. This will help the gang's division." Greta stated as she checked her phone for a text message.

Jo looked at me, but I couldn't read her eyes. Was she scared? Mad? Or worried about me?

A nurse entered the room carrying a driver's license. I snapped a photo. The name read Sergio Lopez, age 18. It listed a Ft. Worth address. I thanked the nurse for her help then we left.

On my way to the office, I called the gang division. I spoke to a friend and gave him what information I had on the shooter. I explained the shooter acted of his own volition when he shot the guy in the emergency room because of his sister. The gang division will handle the notification.

The closer I got to the office, the more tired I became. I wanted to complete my report and head home for sleep. Instead, Jo and I entered the detective's division to a round of applause. Our co-workers heard about our ordeal. We bowed and went to our desk to finish the paperwork.

Once we passed the report to Greta, we headed home for sleep. Tomorrow would be another day. Blood seeped through Jo's bandage. I volunteered to stop by and change it for her, but she stated she had it handled. I didn't argue because I was beat.

It looked as if Madge had been home when I entered the house, but that was past tense. It sits empty now. I laid in bed and contemplated sending a text, but sleep overtook my body. Then dreams came. I saw Jo face to face with a gun time and time again. Then, just when I thought the gun would explode, I awoke in a sweat.

I rolled off the bed and sat on the edge while I thought about my life. Its times like these I question why the military was taken from me, and I still have no answer each time I ask. While I like my job, it's still not the military. I showered before making coffee because I'd been in bed for ten hours and the shower delivers a jolt I needed to walk to the kitchen.

While leaning against the kitchen counter, I texted Jo. She needs to tend to her hand. Then, I shocked myself when I realized Jo came to my mind before Madge. Does that tell me something? I agreed three days ago to work on our marriage. So far, we haven't.

Jo responded to my text with a call. I sat at the kitchen bar, sipping coffee talking to Jo. It was easy. She sent me a picture of her hand, proving that it wasn't bleeding. As we ended our call, Jo reminded me of her doctor's appointment in the morning. She wanted the doctor to release her, but I don't see that happening yet. The gash isn't closed yet.

I still had a few hours before bedtime, so I drove to the gym. It felt good to stretch since my body spent ten hours in bed. While my workout was slow, it was the best in ages. Several guys I see at the gym asked about the hospital incident. I gave them what I could, and that wasn't much.

With hunger pains calling, I drove thru a fast-food restaurant for a grilled chicken salad and enjoyed every bite sitting in the parking lot. By the time I pulled into the drive, Madge was home. Now that I had seen her car, I wasn't sure how happy I was to see it. One thing is for sure, I must decide what to do with my marriage. Do I keep plugging along, or do I sever the ties? With my job, I'd inevitably run into Madge at the hospital. How will that work?

Madge was already in bed when I entered our room. Her hospital iPad was lit up like a Christmas tree. The chart colors glowed in the dark. "I see you are still busy," I stated in a flat tone.

"I performed a complicated surgery today, and the results of the latest scan arrived. Everything looks good. I just hope it stays that way. How are you?" Madge inquired.

"Good. I slept for ten hours, then I went to the gym. Tomorrow I return to the murder investigation." I'm not sure why I elaborated. I shook my head as I walked into the shower because I couldn't sleep with my sweat-soaked body.

When I emerged from the shower, Madge had turned away from me and was softly snoring. Another night without conversation. After we discussed our lack of communication. Is Madge too tired to care anymore?

The following morning, I was awake before my alarm and out the door before Madge turned over. I couldn't handle the tension this early in the day. Jo was on her way to the doctor, and I felt the outcome would disappoint her.

Walking to my desk, Greta called for me. "Hey, Ryker. Grab your coffee and come see me."

I sat across from Greta, and we dove into the murder cases again. "Now that we have Ft. Worth and Dallas with the same MO, what about asking another department? Are you and Jo up for it?"

"I've considered that, and I'd like to ask Houston about their cases. Detective Garcia works down there. I trust him to share his cases without causing a rift. If the killer stays with his same timetable, we have two months to gain as much information about this killer as possible to stop him."

Greta nods in agreement. "I agree with Houston. Do you want to call Garcia? The questions might be better coming from you." Greta suggested with a head tilt.

"I'll call him this morning." I stood and left Greta with her thoughts while I gathered mine.

When I walked into the conference room I studied our board for the umpteenth time. How were we going to find this guy? So far, he's killed in Ft. Worth and Dallas. If Houston has unsolved murders with the same attributes, that means the killer travels. Does he travel for work or simply for his killing habits?

Detective Garcia wasn't in the office when I called, but I left a cryptic message asking for a return call. While I waited, Jo showed with a frown on her face. "No release yet. The doctor gave me a new bandage. It's supposed to stay in place. We'll see. I go back in a few days. If I can get the wound closed, he'll release me."

"We'll work on it. Don't use it, and it'll close." I raised my hand to stop the onslaught of words. "I see the backtalk coming, but it's the only way. How's the hip and arm?"

"They're coming along fine. That's not the doctor's worry." Then, just as Jo finished, my phone rang. It was Detective Garcia. I raised my hand and told her to stay put because she needed to hear this.

I greeted Garcia, and we chatted a minute, then I hit him with my request. Garcia went silent. "Bartley, you called me about unsolved cases, and you want me to stay quiet. What gives?" Garcia asked as it clearly intrigued him.
Without a choice, I divulged our current situation with the murders in Ft. Worth and Dallas. He responded with a low whistle and more silence. "Hold the line while I enter a query. The computer geeks will know I searched for cold cases, but that's all. If you want the files, we'll have to notify the evidence room."

"I understand. I'll take what I can get right now. Then we'll decide what happens." I pleaded because I had a notion Houston has unsolved cases that fit my criteria.

Jo stared at me while I held the phone to my ear. I heard keys tapping on a keyboard and muffled voices in the background. Garcia moaned, and I expected to add unsolved cases to our board.

Garcia returned to the phone. "Bartley, you will not like this, but we have three cases that match your criteria. The oldest is from 2012."

My head bounced as I realized my fears. "Can you give me the preliminaries on the cases? I'll take the information to Commander Huxley, then she'll speak with your commander."

Over the next few minutes, I took notes as Garcia recited the case information. Their murders began in 2012, another followed in 2013, then again in 2018. He'll need to request the case files for the oldest two, but the one in 2018 occurred in November, and the victims were a married couple. Both victims were shot in the head. The man lived long enough to call 911. Unfortunately, he was unconscious when EMS found him, and he died the next day from his injuries. The gathered evidence produced no suspects.

"Thanks, Garcia. This is what I feared. Let me run this past Huxley, and I'll be in touch. You interested in being a task force member? I feel one coming on." I chuckled as I asked.

"With you as the lead, absolutely. I'll have one win on my bedpost." The call ended, and when I turned, Jo grinned.

Then she stated, "so, we add three more murders to our board. I don't see how Greta can keep this quiet for much longer. We'll need a statewide task force if this guy travels the state. What kind of job allows for statewide travel?" Jo's mind went to work as she jotted notes on her pad.

"He owns a company. I'm not sure what kind yet, but I don't see him working for anyone but himself. It would allow him to travel time and time to plan his killings." I stood and headed to Greta's office. When Jo noticed I was missing, she trotted to catch me.

I poked my head in Greta's office, and she knew the outcome of Garcia's call. "Houston has three murders dating back to 2012. Garcia will request the case files on the two oldest murders when we're ready for them. In 2018 the killer shot and killed a couple while they slept in their home. No evidence and no suspects. It sounds like the Rivera's murder." We stood at her desk, waiting.

Greta shuffled papers while putting a plan together. Finally, she looked up at us, "I'll call Garcia's commander. We'll set a meeting with Garcia to discuss their oldest files. Then we'll move to a statewide task force. You two are the leads. Are you ready for it?"

Jo looked at me, and we said in unison, "yes." Excitement wiggled its way into my system when Greta asked us about leading the statewide task force. I've not been a part of one yet, so I'm unsure what to expect, but if I can run a military op, I'll be fine.

We walked back into the conference room with our heads swimming. Jo stood next to the board and added Garcia's cases to our known information. Now, we have unsolved murders in Ft. Worth, Dallas and Houston. Once the recent files made it to the list, we stared at the board. It was overwhelming, but I felt sure we had more coming.

Greta popped into the room and reviewed our notes. Then she commented, "this killer has been active for years, and he would have continued without Ryker spotting the pattern. Austin is next on my list to call. I'll let you know the outcome." She turned and left us with our board.

The day ended with too much information to consider. Will the task force meetings be virtual? Where should we start? I had too many questions with not enough answers.

Jo suggested stopping at our favorite hamburger place, and I couldn't refuse. The burgers are fat and juicy, and the fries are skinny. The cooks use a special seasoning on the meat and the fries. We've tried to get them to tell us their trick, but they just chuckle, and we keep eating.

We discussed the case in between bites. The idea the killer travels is unnerving. He could be anywhere in the state of Texas at any given time. I wondered if he kills outside of Texas. That would definitely make this a federal case, and we'd lose it.

As we left the restaurant, I reminded Jo I'd be by to pick her up in the morning since she wasn't driving until her hand wound closed. She waved.

Jo stood on her porch, waiting for my arrival. She was just as eager as me to get to the office. We hoped Greta calls Austin this morning, so we didn't have to wait all day. Time is of the essence if the killer only murders in July and November. We have one more chance to get him for this year. If we missed him, we'd wait eight long months before another attempt, and I didn't want to wait that long.

Greta stood at our desks when we entered the office. She waved us into her office. My pulse kicked up a notch for reasons unknown. It's too early to have spoken to Austin, so what could she want? Jo thought the same by her facial expression.

We took a seat and watched Greta move papers from one stack to another. "I spoke to Austin overnight, and they have four unsolved cases that match our MO. Their oldest is July 2011. That's ten years of murders. Commander Watts will have their files ready by ten for a discussion. Once we review these, I will implement the task force. You two will present the cases and evidence from each murder to the task force by video, then forward the presentation to each member. You'll coordinate meetings and sending detailed updates to each commander."

I jotted notes as fast as Greta spoke, and I was thankful Jo told me to grab a book. I'm struggling with notetaking. Memory is a strong virtue, but there's always the possibility of missing something. Once Greta excused us, we walked to the conference room. Jo's eyes were enormous. "I expected nothing this big in Ft. Worth. This will be an enormous addition to our resume. If we pull this out, we can go anywhere we want."

"Do you want to leave Ft. Worth, Jo?" I questioned, but I was unsure if I wanted the answer. I didn't wish Jo to go anywhere.

"I don't, but I'm concerned about you, Ryker. With your smarts, and now this, you'll probably get pulled into a thousand different directions from multiple departments. Heck, even the Feds will come calling." Jo stated with a grim look on her face. "I'm not willing to give up the best partner around town." Then her eyes did it again. I struggled to maintain composure.

"Let's get something straight. If I go anywhere, it's a package deal, and I mean that with all my heart. I'm not willing to lose you either. Now that we know where we stand let's get ready for our Austin discussion. Then, we'll have to prepare the presentation, which shouldn't take too much time."

At ten, the trio sat before the video screen, waiting for Commander Watts to connect. A few seconds later, Watts and Detectives Ortega and Brogan appear on the screen. Then, we turned to all business. Ortega seemed to be the lead, and we listened as he recited the characteristics of their cases.

Ortega described the murders as two stabbings, one shooting, and one suffocation. My mind pondered the reasons why the killer changed his method. Was he trying to throw the police off his trail? Or does he enjoy changing things?

Once Ortega concluded his spiel, Commander Watts informed us he would send the files to Greta. We agreed to stay in touch since Greta hasn't announced the task force yet.

Greta suggested we grab lunch while we could since she's planning on announcing the task force at one this afternoon. "I'm inviting each commander to a conference call and letting them know about the task force assignments. I'll stress to keep quiet, but there're no guarantees that'll work. Can you have your presentation ready for ten in the morning? You can share it with the group, then we'll email it to them."

I glanced at Jo, and we both agreed. "Have you decided who's joining our team?"

"Sanchez and Schiller come to mind. What are your thoughts?" Greta inquired as she jotted a note on her pad.

"The sound good to us." We slipped out before she thought of anything else.

While we were away, Greta discussed the situation with Sanchez and Schiller, and they both jumped at the chance to take part. Sanchez and Schiller were partners long before Jo and I. Schiller is older than Sanchez by a decade, but they have the best working relationship. Schiller stands taller than Sanchez, and he doesn't let him forget it. Sanchez thrives on Mexican food while Schiller heads more to Chinese. With these fellows joining the team, we can expect some good laughs.

Jo had a plan in mind about the layout for the presentation. She always went for the clean lines and easy-to-follow designs. We logged into our computers and scrolled through several templates that she'd chosen. I went with her choice.

For the next several hours, we placed the information from each case in the format we'd chosen. Just as we finished, Detective Garcia called with his two oldest file information. He wanted to share one file so bad, he cut me off during my greeting

"Sorry, Ryker, but I can't hold this in any longer. In July 2013, we had a couple die by garrote. The couple slept in their bed, and that's where we found the bodies when the maid found them the following day."

"Wow, Garcia. That's the only other garrote death we've had."

Then Garcia continued, "the other was suffocation in July 2012. A boyfriend found his girl dead in the bed. We worked him over but eventually, we found nothing. No witnesses and no DNA. I'll email the information to you now. We're looking forward to the presentation tomorrow. We'll get him, Ryker."

We ended the call, and I leaned back in my chair. Two deaths using a garrote. Those odds are unbelievable. It flabbergasted Jo too. She quickly added the information to the presentation. So far, we have had fourteen deaths at the hands of one guy. He's been murdering people for a decade that we know of, and we haven't captured him yet.

Greta entered shortly after I finished the call with Garcia. "What's wrong? Both of you look like you've seen a ghost?"

When I explained Garcia's call, Greta paled too. She understood. "We'll get this guy. I promise." Greta fumed and stomped from the room.

After a bit of tweaking, our presentation was complete. We worked on it all afternoon, and the sun was setting by the time we finished. I stepped out of the room for coffee while Jo searched for Greta. We felt she needed to review the presentation before our presenting it. Jo and Greta returned to our room, and Greta cruised through the presentation slide by slide, checking off each murder on her pad.

Jo and I tried to relax by sipping coffee, but it didn't work. Not until Greta put her stamp of approval on it did we enjoy the warm liquid washing down our throats? Greta applauded our abilities. We watched her leave and then we were alone. I wanted supper with Jo, but Madge jumped into my mind for the first time today. Without mentioning supper, I texted Madge. Her reply was quick. She's working late without saying sorry or sending me a frowny face.

I let a little time pass before asking Jo for supper because I didn't want her to think she was my second choice. Because really, she's first. I just haven't figured out how to handle the situation yet. Would Greta make us change partners or precincts? If so, I'll not say anything to anyone because I don't want to lose Jo as a partner.

Chapter 7

The following day I drove Jo to work. She promised her hand wound was better, but I've yet to see it. We were edgy with the morning presentation looming. I'm hoping with the task force members joining us, we'll find additional evidence.

We readied the room for the video meeting, including a whiteboard as Greta brought in coffee. When Sanchez and Schiller arrived, we chatted while we waited for the highly anticipated first task force meeting.

At 9:50, we signed into the video meeting with a host of folks waiting on us. I glanced at Jo, and she read my eyes. We're not the only anxious ones with this assignment.

Promptly at 10:00, Greta started the meeting. First, she explained the reason behind the statewide task force, and then she had everyone introduce themselves. We went last, and she introduced Jo and me as the lead detectives for this assignment.

The presentation began with an overview of each murder dating back to 2011. A few questions arose, but nothing earth-shattering. Next, the group discussed ideas about the killer's work habits. They agree with us that the killer crossed paths with these people. But we still had no answer on how.

Once the presentation ended, Greta asked me to share my profile. I wasn't prepared for that discussion, but Jo was, so she grabbed my book and passed it to me. I gave her a slight grin in return. Then she whispered a reminder to tell them the pattern. At that, I raised my eyebrow.

I shared my profile with the team by adding a disclaimer that I'm no profiler, but I felt the killer's profile was fairly straightforward. "He's in his 30s to 40s, divorced, controlling or bossy, highly intelligent, probably owns a company because of the ability to travel. I suspect he met his victims through work, but that's not confirmed. If he owns a company, he's your typical looking guy, with short hair, no facial hair or visible tattoos. He might have tattoos, but they're in inconspicuous places, so he can cover them when the need arises."

As I sipped coffee, I studied the faces of each task force member. They were in awe. "Stop me if you have questions. There's one more item I'd like to share." I glanced at Greta and Jo, and both nodded. The members watched the exchange, and they seemed to sit up taller in their chairs. They anticipated a bombshell.

We flipped the whiteboard over, showing the dates of deaths and the corresponding weekday. I heard gasps as their brains received the information. Then, I explained the pattern. Each person on the call admitted they would have never picked up on the pattern. One guy, Detective Brown from Houston, asked how I knew the day of the week for a past calendar date. Or what drew that information out? I grinned and answered, "that's a story for another day. Now that you've heard the cases, studied the pattern, what are your initial thoughts? I realize this information is new to you, so I get it if you need to think about it."

Detective Morton, a large African American guy, made the first comment. "I think something happened to our killer during July and November. Maybe he got divorced, or someone died. Is that your same thinking point, Bartley?"

Jo and Greta nodded yes, while I replied, "absolutely, I do. Personally or professionally, something happened to him that caused him to jump to murder and only during those months. I can't answer how he contains his desire to kill during the stagnant months yet, but we will."

We gave the group time to speak amongst themselves, then Greta called the group back together. "Our suggestion is to review your cases from start to finish. This group will meet twice a week, but the lines of communication remain open 24/7. If something happens, so does a meeting."

With no further comments, the first task force meeting ended. It felt good knowing ten people worked on this assignment. Chances are, with all of our experience combined, we should catch this guy before he kills again.

Greta thanked Jo and me for an excellent presentation and for divulging the pattern and profile. I shrugged my shoulders because, for me, it was no big deal.

Sanchez and Schiller accepted the two oldest cases from 2011 and 2015 from Greta. She requested them to review all evidence and photos. If there were witnesses, Greta wants them spoken to again. Then, she passed the files from 2018 and the Rivera murders to us and requested the same. "There's something in these files we're missing. I expect you to find it."

We watched as Greta grabbed her things and headed out the door. That left the four of us staring at each other. Detective Sanchez cleared his throat. "Bartley, your profile, and the pattern information is unbelievable. We're stepping out for lunch, then we'll start on our two cases. Thanks for your insights."

"I'm glad you both agreed to participate. We'll catch this guy and put him away forever."

Once they left the room, Jo and I grinned at each other. She stated, "that went fantastic. You're a natural speaker, even though you don't enjoy doing it. You blew those guys away with your input." She stood and walked to me. "Let's go eat. I'm starving now that is over."

We turned off the lights in our room and left the office. The weather turned cloudy and windy. Maybe a little rain would come calling this afternoon. With the sun tucked behind the clouds, we opted for our favorite food truck. We talked of anything but the case. That would come later because this case will consume our lives until we capture this killer.

Jo mentioned Madge in passing, so I felt I owed her an explanation. I told her everything, the conversation Madge and I had, and then what's happened since. Jo lifted an eyebrow and studied my face. "That's right, I haven't seen Madge since the triple shooting and our brief encounter at the hospital. For all I know, she hasn't been home."

I paused because I expected questions. When I didn't get any, I took Jo by the hand, and we went back to work. With Sanchez and Schiller working on two files, we took the Rivera's case and the other one from 2018. The Rivera's case we knew by heart, so we started with the murder in 2018. We glanced at it earlier when Greta sent us the files, but now, we have the time to review everything, including photos and lab evidence.

Jo laid the file information on the table. There were stacks of photos. We started with them. If we saw something that warranted a closer look, we noted it. Our 2018 case occurred in July. Someone entered the victim's home then shot and killed him. The man lived in a nice Ft. Worth neighborhood that Jo labeled as middle class. He took pride in his home and his lawn. No DNA inside the house. One exterior photo showed a sticker in the lower left of the dining room window. But when Jo enlarged the picture, the decal was indecipherable. "Ryker, the sticker looks red and yellow. Do we know of a security company that uses red and yellow in their logo?"

"Not right off hand, I don't. Did we see a security panel in the photos?" I asked Jo, and something niggled my brain.

Jo reached over and grabbed a stack of pictures. She thumbed through a few when she handed me one. "Is that a control panel on the wall? If it is, the door cuts off a portion."

I reached for the picture and the magnifying glass at the same time. Jo chuckled when I dropped both. She leaned over, "one at a time, Ryker. It makes life easier."

After I had them in my hands, her statement caused me to pause. Was Jo referring to the picture and the glass or her and Madge? Either way, it made sense.

The picture was darker than most in the stack, but I surmised the square box was an alarm panel. We searched the other images and found no other box. I assumed every house had two, one for the owner's suite and the other close to an exterior door. I jotted that tidbit on my pad for later.

"Let's compare the Rivera's file with this one and see if a commonality exists." For the next several minutes, we discussed this possibility, but eventually, we found none. The Rivera's lived on the ritzier side of town. The Rivera's were married where our 2018 victim was single. He had never been married, and he had no kids that we could find.

"Look at this, Ryker. We didn't think to the check on the fibers." Of course, as soon as Jo said it, I jumped up.

"That's it. That's what I forgot. I jotted that note on a pad in my car. I wanted to compare the 2018 fiber with the fiber found at the Rivera's. If they are a match, we have confirmation of the same killer."

While Jo looked over my shoulder, we compiled an email to the lab requesting a comparison between the fibers from both crime scenes. Then we waited.

Jo waved a square plastic holder in the air. "Here's a CD of the crime scene, too. Are you up for watching a video?"

"I'm grabbing a coffee before we start. Can I get you one?"

"Absolutely. I'll have it ready to start when you return." Jo stated as she removed the CD from the case.

Jo was true to her word. I entered the room with two steaming cups of coffee, and she sat at the laptop waiting to push the start button. We sipped our coffee while watching the crime scene unfold before us.

Neither one took notes, instead, we watched the scene. We listened intently to the video maker and their take on the scene.

Then, we replayed it, taking notes along the way. The video maker enters the home by the front door. He records an image of each room, showing no disturbances. The owner's suite showed a different picture as the man lay in bed sleeping when the intruder entered his home, shot and killed him. Then the video pans the room from the doorway before turning to the victim.

The man lay on his back while he slept. An indentation in the carpet led the detectives to surmise the killer stood two to three feet away from the victim when he fired the shot. They later found a fiber in the indentation. They found no casing. There was blood spatter on the wall behind and to the side of the bed.

After the video maker leaves the owner's suite, he moves to the windows and doors then to the outside. He records each window, inside and out, showing no signs of tampering. The same goes for the outside of each exterior door. Then, he walks alongside the house's perimeter, searching for footprints, and finds none.

Once the video ends for the second time, we turn to the notes. Jo reads, "a co-worker found the body when he didn't show for a meeting. The victim was a financial planner. From the autopsy, the bullet was so mangled they could not match it. They guess the bullet to be a 9 MM or a 380 caliber."

I paused before I started, "the killer is determined not to get caught, but yet he shoots people, knowing bullets are traceable. He stands away from the victim when shooting them, yet he holds the person when he uses a garrote. I wonder what a psychologist would say about this man. Would they label him a psychopath?"

"They might, Ryker. Think about it. Psychopaths are typically bold, lack empathy, and like violence. It could be his genetic makeup or triggered by environmental factors."

As I thought about Jo's remarks, I glanced at the whiteboard. "It's environmental for this guy." If I knew what happened to him in July and November, we could find him. Wonder how many deaths, marriages and divorces Texas has in July and November of any given year? I doodled as this idea simmered in my mind. Is there a database that holds this information? Another note for my pad.

My email alert sounded, bringing me back to the moment. I rolled my chair to my laptop and clicked the email icon open. Detective Cabello's email sat highlighted in a list of unopened emails. I opened it, then smiled.

"Cabello forwarded us the 2015 fiber results. I'm sending it along to the lab for comparison with our Rivera and 2018 fibers. Hopefully, we'll get a match from this." I typed my email then sent it on its way. We heard a commotion outside our door. When it got closer, we realized Schiller and Sanchez were walking our way.

Schiller knocked on our office door. Jo snickered. "Come in, Schiller. You don't need to knock." She grins because he looks like a kid. He stills carries a baby face.

"I'm glad both of you are here. We have a crime scene video from 2011 on a small tape, but we don't know how to watch it. Do you?" He hands the small cassette to Jo.

"This, Schiller is a camcorder cassette. Sanchez should know this too. Anyway, the lab has a tape deck that will play these. I'll call down there and have them bring us one." Jo stepped to the room's corner to make her plea while the three of us talked about the case.

"Guys, Jo and I watched the video from the 2018 crime scene. There wasn't much there. The only disturbed room was the owner's suite, where the victim died. There was a fiber found in the carpet indentation where they surmised the shooter stood.

No footprints outside and no signs of forced entry on the windows or doors."

Sanchez spoke, "our killer has one goal, and that's killing."

"Interesting point of view, Sanchez," I replied as I considered his statement.

Jo returned to the group. "The lab is sending a tape deck. It will be here shortly." Then, just as she finished, a younger guy entered the room.

"I'm here with the tape deck. Do you need help to connect to your laptop?" The guy's eyes roamed the room.

We answered, "yes." Then he chuckled.

I spoke, "connect it to this one. Can we keep it for a few days? We have old cases we're working on."

"Sure. Sign this form. We have no waiting list for it. Besides, we have three others downstairs collecting dust. Here you go."

We watched as the guy gave us the instructions on connecting the tape deck to a laptop and then operating it. We felt accomplished after that ordeal.

I slid the cassette into the tape deck and waited. The picture was small and grainy, but we got through it. This crime scene was the first one in Ft. Worth that we suspected from our killer. There was one other case in Austin in 2011. This victim was a college-aged girl who lived in a condo in downtown Ft. Worth. She fought her attacker while the killer stabbed her multiple times. The killer found her in the bed when the attack began. Blood stains on the bedspread give the impression she moved to the far side of the bed, then she scrambled to get away from her attacker by tracking blood into the bathroom. That's where he caught her and ended her life. Pools of blood sat on her white rugs in front of the sink. But the killer returned her body to the bed. Why?

The video shows the back door locked from the inside and no forced entry signs on the windows or the front door. I stopped the video, "did anyone hear the detective mention the garage door? I didn't."

"No, Ryker, I didn't," Jo answered. Then the other two guys shook their heads from side to side. That's frustrating. If you're already at the scene, why not examine everything since we have only one chance at this.

"Swell." I restarted the video. Then I jotted a note to review the autopsy.

Once the video ended, Sanchez asked, "did the victim work? Could that be our connection?"

Jo shook her head as she replied, "we haven't found a correlation between jobs. The victims seem to be of all ethnicities and work in different industries."

Thinking about the stickers, I asked, "do we have a video of the exterior of the home? or a photo of it? I'm looking for a widow decal like for a security company?" Everyone glanced over their notes, then they picked up the photos.

Sanchez raised his hand, "I think this is it, but the distance is so great, I can't tell the company." He passed the photo to me. I used a magnifying glass, and that didn't help either. This one might have been a red, white and blue decal, but I wasn't even sure about that.

"Why the concern with the security system, Ryker?" Schiller asked. He was an intelligent detective but young.

I paused as I worked to put my thoughts in order. "We noticed a window sticker at the Rivera's home. That led me to notate each murder scene's security decal. It might mean nothing, but I'm covering everything I see and know about a particular scene. But that brings up a question. If these murder victims have a security system, why wasn't it turned on at the time of the killer's entry? The Rivera's was off too."

Jo stated, "we didn't call the security company to find out what time someone turned it off."

Schiller spoke, "I like that, Samples. Did the killer turn it off before he entered, and if he did, how?"

Jo looked at me, and I grinned. I liked that angle. Now, I wanted to know if every murder victim had a window decal or yard placard. Then, I want to know if the system was on at the time of the killer's entry.

I shared my idea with the group. Sanchez and Schiller agreed and will ask about their cases. I know those will be most difficult to find out because of the age of the crime, but it's worth the effort.

While I had it on my mind, I emailed the task force with a request to follow up on the security systems for each victim. Was there an active system in the home at the time of the murder? Also, was the alarm set? If the victim had an alarm, which company serviced it?

We reviewed our two files, and both victim's homes sported red and yellow window decals. Next, Jo searched the internet for the company. It took Jo a few clicks to land on the website for the security company. They specialize in residential and commercial security systems, both wired, and wireless.

I called the company from my landline, hoping it would prove I'm at the Ft. Worth Police Department. Before someone answered my call, I tapped the speakerphone button. Jo and I hovered over the phone as we listened to it ring.

After eight rings, a lady answered. I stated my name, and then I asked for a manager. The lady was polite when she stated she was their answering service because they closed early today. She continued when she said they would open at eight in the morning.

I wrote the security company's number on my pad then circled it in heavy red marks. Jo chuckled. "Don't want to forget that call, Ryker?" Jo rolled back to her desk.

Then, she stood and went to the whiteboard. She added the decal color for each crime scene she knew. Standing back from the board, she viewed her handiwork. Our two Ft. Worth murders had red and yellow decals, while both earlier murders showed red, white and blue stickers. Sanchez and Schiller will provide their results.

"Ryker, you can take me home. There's nothing else for us to do today. Tomorrow we will concentrate on the security company angle." Jo gathered her things while I sat at the table.

"I'm hungry. Can we stop for supper?" I watched Jo work through the idea. She wanted to turn me down, but she didn't.

"If you're sure, then yes, I'm hungry too." Jo plopped her bag on her desk and searched for her lipstick. If she's stopping for supper, she must be presentable. When she found it, she applied her favorite summer color, hot pink. Then she took her pick and ran it through her hair a few times.

I watched the show as Jo readied herself for the world. It was amazing. Who wouldn't want to be seen with Jo on their arm? Her skin is a creamy coffee color with high cheekbones. I turned my head, so I found something else to grab my attention while she finished.

That didn't work, so I stood and gathered my things. The last thing I saw as we left the office was the note circled in red.

We climbed into my car, and Jo peeked at her hand. "You're going to like this hand. It's closed. I have another doctor's appointment in the morning, so I'll be late. I can drive myself." Jo gave me a sideways glance. In a way, it's sad she can drive because I won't need to pick her up for the morning trip to the office. I'll have to wait to see her smiling face.

I nodded as an answer because I used the traffic as a distraction. Then, it wasn't an excuse. We came to a screeching halt right before we crossed a major intersection. We stopped as the second car in line, then we heard a massive collision. Car parts showered our car. Jo and I jumped from our car and ran to the accident without a second's delay.

The accident scene was horrific. Three vehicles met in the intersection, with one being a massive concrete truck. The truck struck an SUV in the driver's door and spun it several times before it came to rest. Jo ran to the SUV while I checked on a pickup truck driver sitting across the intersection from us. The concrete truck struck the pickup truck in the left front quarter. The truck driver waved me off, so I turned and ran to Jo's side.

When I saw Jo, I knew the seriousness of the situation just escalated. Jo yelled, "Ryker, I can't get a pulse on the mom."

"Mom?" Then I turned my head and saw the little boy sitting in the back seat with eyes as wide as saucers. "Hey, little man, my name is Ryker. We're here to help you and your mom. Okay." I reached my hand back and patted his knee. His eyes moved, but he made no sound.

I watched Jo rub her balled fist into the driver's chest. We heard a moan. EMS, fire trucks and police cars roared to our location and squealed to a stop. I stepped away and spoke to the Ft. Worth Fire Department Captain. "Captain. The mom is in rough shape. She lost a pulse, but Jo brought her back. There's a baby in the car." The captain moaned that time.

The captain barked instructions to his crew, and the driver laid on the gurney within minutes of their arrival. She was semi-conscious and asked about the baby, not her baby. Jo caught on quicker than I did.

Jo leaned over the driver, "are you the baby's mom?"

The patient shook her head and said his contact information was in a diaper bag. I bolted for the car and searched for the bag. It was lying on its side on the floorboard. A police officer held the little boy while I pilfered the bag. Once I had the card, I called the mom's number. She answered on the first ring, and while I explained my call, I heard a door close. Then, she said to give her twenty minutes, and she'd meet us at the emergency room.

We loaded the driver and the baby into the ambulance and watched as they pulled away. The driver reached over and held the little boy's hand. He never cried or smiled. I prayed he suffered no injury while the driver's injuries were visibly substantial.

After the patients left the scene, we did too. Police officers cleared the way for us to scoot around the debris field. Jo didn't talk for a while after that ordeal. I left her to her thoughts. But when we turned the corner to our favorite restaurant, I got a grin.

"That was awful, Ryker. I hope the baby is okay. Unfortunately, the driver, who I assume was the boy's nanny, sustained a serious injury to her left leg. She's so young. I hope it doesn't impair her mobility."

"All I can say is we were supposed to be there at that time. It's because of you that girl is still living. No one else ran to help." I sighed when I thought of how people are standoffish these days. No one wants to involve themselves anymore. "Let's eat, then home. Tomorrow is the day your doctor releases you to full duty. I feel it."

Chapter 8

I entered the office alone as Jo drove herself to her doctor's appointment. Around midnight I heard the doorknob rattle. Madge made it home, but I fell asleep as soon as I knew she was safely inside. My day started before hers, and I left her sleeping with a half pot of coffee waiting.

My desk sat untouched, and the first thing catching my attention was the red circle. After pouring a cup of coffee, I sat and grabbed the phone. I dialed the number for the security company with the red and yellow logo.

A man answered on the second ring. After I explained my reason for calling, he referred me to the manager, Mr. Priestly. While I waited for the call to transfer, I centered the documents so they would be ready for the dates of interest. Then, just as I sipped my coffee, Mr. Priestly came on the line.

Swallowing in a hurry is sometimes painful, but I made it work. I explained my call again, and there was a pause in our conversation. Mr. Priestly asked a few questions then said he'd return the call once he had the information. I couldn't ask for anything more than that.

I turned on my computer so I could check emails while I finished my coffee. My text messages sounded. I fully intended to receive one from Jo with a notice of release. Instead, it was from Madge. Her text was about the car accident victim. My reply stated we were at the scene. I asked about the driver. She sustained multiple injuries, including a lacerated spleen, and a broken leg, requiring surgery. Then I asked about the little boy, and I grinned when Madge texted his parents took him home overnight without a scratch. That news made my day.

Jo bounced into the office as I finished with Madge. The doctor released her to full duty, but she must maintain a covering over the hand for a while since it's not completely closed. Then she asked about my smile.

Once I explained about the nanny's recovery and the baby, we exchanged a high five. Then we turned to all business because we had a serial killer to catch. I updated Jo on the security company, and the manager will call us back with our requested information.

"Ryker, I feel good about the security companies. But I can't explain why."

My phone rang, and I grabbed it, hoping for a return call from Mr. Priestly. Instead, Detective Ortega called. I listened as he explained the results of the security company contacts. The murder cases in 2011 and 2013 were too old to retrieve any viable information on them. Then, Ortega asked if we contacted the company with the red and yellow sticker. When I confirmed, he asked us to add his murder in November 2019 to the list. The company should provide information on that one with it being recent. Then he explained one murder in July 2019 had no security system. He reviewed the notes, and the victim had moved into her apartment forty-five days prior because a tornado destroyed her home.

Then Ortega gave us a surprise. The lady had an appointment to meet someone the day before her death, but no one knew who she was meeting. Her boyfriend provided that tidbit and added she kept her calendar on her cell phone, which Ortega found at the bottom of the evidence box.

"Ortega, that's a solid lead for us. Send the phone to your lab and see if they can retrieve her calendar for us. I'd like to hear the results too as soon as you have them."

We ended our call, and a thought came to mind. I wondered for how long security companies keep their customer list and system information. With Ortega's call, we need to compile a list of the security companies.

I rehashed the information with Jo once she returned from meeting Greta. "Jo, we need to compile a list of security companies for our victims. Someone needs to contact each company."

"I'll start on that now. Ortega gave us good news with the victim's cell phone calendar. I just hope she didn't abbreviate the company. That could prove tedious work to decipher." Jo logged into her computer and prepared the worksheet for the security companies.

We added our victims to the list first, then Ortega's. To add Dallas and Houston, we had to dig through our notes and find the pictures to support what we remembered. We had a few cases where we had no mention of a security system. Dallas in 2014, and Austin in 2019.

Greta strolled over to our office as she spoke to the other detectives under her command. "I have a thought, but I wanted to run it by you two first. We've solicited cases from the largest cities, but we haven't asked the rest of the state. Should we?"

Jo glanced at me, and I looked at Greta. "I would suggest we ask the state. The more knowledge we have, the better our chances of capturing this guy."

"I'll handle today." Greta turned and left without another word. I watched her go and wondered why she didn't ask for an update.

"What's bothering you, Ryker? You look perplexed." Jo inquired.

"Greta didn't ask for an update. That's strange. Wonder what's going on with her?" I pondered on it for a few seconds. Then I returned my attention to the company list.

I dialed Dallas Detective Cabello about his July 2014 murder because we couldn't locate a security sticker on the windows. When he answered, I explained my call, then I heard him shuffle papers as he searched for the answer. "Our female victim lived in an upscale neighborhood. She retired from pharmaceutical sales and moved into the home two months before her death. Someone suffocated her while she slept. The medical examiner determined the date of death as Sunday, but a concerned neighbor did not find her until Thursday. Another neighbor reported a white van at the victim's house, but then they retracted their statement because of the angle of their home to the victims. They were unsure if the van was in our victim's drive or her next-door neighbor's."

Since we had no questions for Cabello, we ended the call and added the information to our list. Once Jo entered the new information, we studied the list. The list gave us interesting information by showcasing the security companies with the most victims. The company logos of red and yellow and yellow and green are the most predominant. Then, one with a yellow and blue logo, followed by a red, white and blue logo. Our cases in 2011 and 2015 had a red, white and blue decal on the windows. If we were lucky, the 2015 case might provide us usable information.

"I'll call the red, white and blue company when I find a number." Jo searched the internet for the logo but found no matches. She returned to the search screen and perused the articles associated with the security company. Further down the page, Jo found another company that purchased the security company that uses the red and yellow logo. There was no mention of the owner's name.

"Ryker, our red and yellow company, purchased the red, white and blue security company two years ago. So when Mr. Priestly returns your call, you can ask him about it."

I nodded my head in acknowledgment as I stood from my chair. "It's lunchtime. Are you ready? I don't want to sit here all day waiting for Mr. Priestly to call."

Jo walked to the door, then looked back at me. "Come on, Ryker."

We climbed into my car in silence. Then Jo broke it, "I guess you saw Madge last night since you knew about the car accident victim."

"Actually, I didn't. She came home late in the night, but I didn't see her. I left before she got up. I guess she felt guilty because we didn't speak yesterday, so texted me this morning about the accident. When I told her we were at the scene, she said, you saved that girl." I glanced at Jo, and a smile spread across her face.

"That was an amazing feeling. To know she wasn't breathing, then to have her wake enough to communicate was something special." Jo described her feelings with a faraway look. She never mentioned Madge again.

We ate and discussed the murders. Every day that passed meant we were one day closer to the next kill. No one wanted to see that happen. We couldn't pinpoint the connection between these victims. While we know the same person crossed paths with each of these people, we just had to find the path that led to the killer. Once we know it, we'll capture him and put him away forever.

After our return to the office, Jo worked on the cases while I helped a fellow officer with another crime ring. These targets upscale shopping districts. We mapped the crimes on paper, then I read each report. I glared at the map and information on the officer's desk, then I circled the area in red, just like I did for Officer Hutton.

Jo was typing away on her laptop when I entered the office, so I didn't interrupt. But when she continued, I finally gave in to curiosity. "What are you doing, Jo?"

"I'm cleaning up our list. I've added the victim's addresses, city, victim gender, method of death, decal color, and any known evidence to our report. It will help us when we need a quick reference. I'm almost finished." She glanced at me when my phone rang.

Greta called me, letting us know she had two more cases associated with our killer. One case is south of Plano, and the other is west of Wichita Falls. She'll have the files to us by morning. When the call ended, I looked at Jo, "you can add two rows to your worksheet. Greta found two more cases that fit out the killer. We should have the files in the morning."

"Two more. We have too many as it is with our current number." Jo clicked the keys adding two rows for tomorrow's files.

Glancing at my phone, I moaned because Mr. Priestly hadn't returned my call. It's midafternoon, and I wondered why it takes so long for him to gather the information. He runs a security company, so his records should be on his computer.

In my mind, I gave him another hour, and then I'd call him. I need to add to his list anyway with Ortega's case in Austin. Also, the crime lab hasn't called about fibers either.
"Jo, did we find security system panels in each home? I know we found a few, but what if the window decals were for show and not actual service? How would someone know that information?"

I watched as Jo swung her head from side to side. She didn't have the answer either. Then she added, "what other companies or services could touch each of our victims?"

"Are you suggesting a salesman, pest control, etc.? If so, that list could be endless." I said as I rubbed my neck, trying to find a link.

"Think about it. Our victims live all over Texas, and they work in different industries, or they're retired. The only idea that fits is the service industry. It's someone that travels and offers their services to others. I thought about insurance sales, but that's done over the phone more now than in the past. Pest control companies are more local, as is appliance repair. That left residential roofers and construction companies. Then, I thought about security companies. Do they travel a state for opportunities to sell their service?"

I took a moment to consider her ideas. "Jo, you might be right. Let me study on that one for a bit."

Sitting at my desk, I pilfered the photos of the scenes. It didn't matter which scene I studied. I found security system panels in most. So, what does that tell me about the ones without? Was the victim in the market for a security system?

My phone rang, and I answered. Relief washed over my body as Mr. Priestly identified himself. He found our requested information. The Rivera's deactivated their security system at 2:00 am while the one in July 2018 was turned off at 2:30 am. Mr. Priestly continued by saying someone from inside the home deactivated the systems.

I jotted notes to keep the information fresh. "Mr. Priestly, does your report show the times the systems were activated for each address?"

"Sure. Your July date shows activated at 10:00 pm while the other was 11:02 pm." Then Mr. Priestly waited for me to gather my thoughts. "Is there any other information you need, Detective?"

"Actually, there is. We have another case in Austin for November 2019 with the same red and yellow logo. Can you check on that one? Also, we heard that your company purchased another security system company that bore a red, white, and blue logo. Do you have their old records?"

Mr. Priestly cleared his throat. "I owned that company with the described logo. Conner Piston bought me out when my wife died, then he gave me a job with his company. You say someone is murdering people in their homes, and it relates to the security systems."

"We're looking into it. Oddly, our Ft. Worth victims deactivated their alarms during the night of their murder. Wouldn't you agree that's odd?" I waited this time. It took so long for the man to reply. I thought he hung up on me.

"If you put it like that, it seems odd. I'll search for my old records. Can you give me the dates and addresses? Once I have it, I'll call back."

I provided Mr. Priestly the information he needed to search his records. Then I rehashed my notes.
Conner Piston is the company owner that sports the yellow and red logo, and he also purchased the red, white, and blue company. The original owner of the red, white and blue company now works for Conner Piston. I nodded because it's strange how things happen in life.
As I glanced away from my notes, I noticed Jo staring at me with an eyebrow raised. "So, what did you find out? You were on the phone for a while."

Over the next few minutes, I recounted the conversation with Mr. Priestly. Jo's eyes grew wide when I shared about the company purchase. When I finished, she looked at her notes. "Just to clarify, someone from inside the house turned off both security systems on the nights of the murders. That's not a coincidence. It can't be."

"I agree. Mr. Priestly will call me with the information on Ortega's case and ours from 2015. If they show someone from inside turned them off as well, we have a pattern. And I don't like it. I'll wait for Mr. Priestly's call before updating the team.

The sun slid down, and the skies grew darker as we sat in our office brainstorming ideas. Finally, we set a video meeting with the task force. They deserved more than an email with the latest information. We would notify the group in the morning of our afternoon meeting.

Jo and I left the office together, and I followed her from the lot. It was nicer when we rode together. I peeked at my phone for text messages. There were none. I guess I would be home alone again tonight. So, I considered my supper options when an idea came to me. I would stop at the gym for a quick workout before heading home. That notion boosted my mood.

Once I sweated out my frustration, I climbed into my car for the second trip of the night. I was hungry, but I needed protein, so I hit a drive-thru at one of the local shops for chicken. By the time I made it home, I had devoured the chicken with room in my stomach for something else. Just as I pulled into the garage, Madge's garage door opened.

I waited for her to exit the car and grab her gear from the back seat. We greeted one another with a peek on the cheek. She sniffed me, "you have first dibs on the shower." Then chuckled as she entered the house. I followed her inside then I headed upstairs for a much-needed shower. When I returned downstairs, Madge sat on the sofa with her feet tucked underneath her, studying someone's medical test. I know not to bother her when she's in that zone.

When ice cubes crashed into my glass, Madge glanced at me. Her expression could have been mad or just concerned. Either way, she didn't look happy. Then she said, "the car driver in the accident the other day has more injuries than we originally thought. She'll need another leg surgery and possibly another after that. I feel so bad for this girl. She's in college struggling to finish her degree, now that's been put on hold."

"That is sad, but at least it's a temporary setback, right? She'll recover, won't she?" I questioned.

"I hope so, Ryker, I hope so." Madge laid her iPad on the table as she struggled to escape work. Then she looked at me, "have you ever been so sleepy that you can't fall asleep? That's me. I can't remember the last time I slept for eight hours straight."

I stood behind Madge and massaged her shoulders. There were so many knots I couldn't fathom a count. As time passed, the knots decreased, and tension subsided. Madge moaned. "Why don't you try to sleep? Leave your work downstairs for the night. I'll sleep down here because I'm leaving early in the morning for a task force meeting."

Madge stood and wrapped her arms around my neck. We gazed into each other's eyes, and then we kissed. A kiss that I expected to feel different. We hadn't kissed like that in a month, and I expected sparks to fly, but that wasn't the case. Madge felt it too, as we separated, and she turned her eyes downward.

"Maybe, I'm too tired, Ryker. I'll see you tomorrow." With that, Madge left me standing in the family room, wondering where this leaves us? The sparks we once had, are no longer there. Are we holding on to false hope that our relationship can survive?

When morning came, I slipped out of the house without waking Madge. As I laid on the sofa late into the night, pondering our relationship, I heard her feet pattering in our bathroom around 1:00 am. She needed sleep, but I needed answers. Madge must know I'm not living like this forever. She'll have to choose the hospital or me, and I know that isn't fair, but I didn't marry her just to be married. I married her to have a life partner, someone to share things with, and I can't do that if we never see each other.

On my drive to the office, I didn't even turn on the radio. I drove in silence except for the occasional car horn. Instead, I concentrated on myself and what today might bring the team. We have a promising lead with the security companies.

When I entered the office, Jo greeted me with a smile and a large cup of coffee. Jo's eyes did that thing again. I could tell she had questions, but she held her tongue. She knows I'll talk when I can, and that time is growing closer.

Instead of questions, we walked into our temporary office together and found Greta waiting for us. We exchanged glances, as neither of us expected this.

Greta asked, "what time is your task force meeting? I want to make sure I'm available."

Jo looked at me, and I rattled off, "11 or 1, depending on the team and your schedule too." I grinned because I felt awkward, and I couldn't explain why. Was something up with Greta?

Returning the smile, Greta replied, "either time works for me."

We watched her leave, then I got signed into my email and began typing my meeting request. I suggested 11 first because I didn't want to wait until after lunch. The sooner we meet, the sooner we get direction on the case.

Once I emailed, we waited. Everything is hurried up, then wait. I thumbed through my reminders from yesterday, and I spotted Mr. Priestly's name. He should call back today with additional information too.

"Jo, can you pull backgrounds on Conner Piston and Joseph Priestly. Mr. P sold his company to Conner, and I want to see how they stand financially. While I feel Mr. Priestly is too old to carry out the murders, Conner isn't. He's in his middle forties. Before I call him for an interview, I want his background."

"I'll do it now while we wait." Jo agreed to handle my request. I could have done it myself, but I know Jo, and she likes to feel needed. And she is.

Just as I sipped my coffee, my phone rang. I answered, thinking it was a team member, but it wasn't. Instead, Mr. Priestly returned my call. I thanked him for his prompt attention, hoping to ease his mind.

"Detective Bartley, I researched all the dates you presented. We'll start oldest and work forward. The date in 2011 was too old to find any record. The alarm for 2015 was deactivated at 2:30 am from the inside. On July 11, 2017, there were no alarm service notes for that date and address."

I thought about his last statement, "but there was a red and yellow sticker in the window."

Mr. Priestly grimaced, and I heard keys tapping, then a moan. "We had their service for years, but they called a week before requesting to cancel their service because they were moving to another security company. They didn't tell us the name of the new company. My report on July 11, 2018 shows the alarm was turned off from the inside at 2:00 am while someone deactivated the system in Austin on November 2019 from the inside at 2:35 pm."

"So why would the residents deactivate their alarms in the middle of the night? That makes little sense." I couldn't fathom a logical explanation for this scenario. It doesn't work.

Mr. Priestly asked, "Detective if you don't mind me asking, why are you concentrating on us? You don't suspect someone from our company would murder these people."

"Right now, we're gathering all the information we can about our victims. Window decals gave us the lead, and that's what we're following. The murders occurred in different cities throughout Texas, so someone crossed their paths. That's the someone we're tracking. Do you know of anyone acting strange at your company? I haven't spoken to the owner yet, Conner Piston."

Silence on the other end. I waited. Finally, Mr. Priestly stated, "Conner bought my business when I needed help. My wife passed after a cancer battle, and I needed the money to survive. Then he gave me a job. There is no way Conner is a killer."

"Ok. If not Conner, is there anyone else at your company that seems out of sorts or bothered?"

"Not that comes to mind. Do you think the killer hacks into our computer system then turns off the victim's alarms while the reports show it as an inside job? I wouldn't think many people know that's possible."

Now, I paused. "Wait. That's possible, Mr. Priestly. The killer hacks into a main computer system, turns the alarm system off, enters the home, then leaves without detection. What about motion sensors? Are those controlled in the same manner?"

"Yes, everything connected in the home would be controlled in the same manner. Over the last ten years, technology advances allowed the operation of security system controls from the main computer system. But, generally, if someone deactivates the system from another computer, the reports show the same. Someone would have to be far more intelligent than I to log into the primary system to manipulate a report."

"Sorry to keep you on the line, Mr. Priestly, but this is valuable information. How would someone gain enough knowledge about a company's computer to hack into it?" I jotted notes on my pad as I heard my email alert sound.

"For that, I'm not sure. Conner could explain that part for you. When I had my company, we didn't depend on computers to track our information. We had people work 24/7, operating the phones. Nowadays, computers do it all." He sighed, and he thought about my situation. "If you have any more questions, let me know. Otherwise, I'm late for a staff meeting."

"Thanks for your time, Mr. Priestly. It's been very beneficial." I returned the handset to the cradle and stared at Jo.

"We have more information. I'm convinced our killer works in the security industry. We just have to find him." I grinned.

I clicked open my emails, and the team agreed to meet at eleven. Not only did I have the information on
the murders, I had knowledge of how the killer gained access to the victim's residences. I called for Greta because she needed to hear this before the meeting.

Greta and Jo sat before me in our office, both look at the anticipation on their faces. Jo played with her earring while Greta worked her jaw. Over the next twenty minutes, I rehashed my call with Mr. Priestly by detailing his information from the murders then covering the idea of our killer hacking into security systems to gain entry undetected.

No one offered a comment. They sat in silence, pondering my conversation. Greta jumped first, "so, you think the killer works at a security company, and he hacks into a victim's security account, turns it off, does his deed, then leaves. But when the company runs their reports, it shows the alarm deactivated from inside the house." She shook her head from side to side as this was unbelievable.

How long did it take the killer to figure this one out?

"That's exactly what I think. After our team meeting this morning, our concentration turns to security companies. We need backgrounds on every security company involved. It will be difficult to find anything on the company from 2011 since the sticker is blurry. But we'll do what we can with the others." I looked at Jo for some sort of response. This shocked her.

"If this is true, not only does our killer work in the security business, he also knows computers. This guy is intelligent, and that's scary." Jo stated as she stared holes through me.

Greta chuckled, then said, "well, if he's that smart, he better look out. Ryker is smarter. He can spot things the rest of us can't. That's what makes him invaluable. All killers think they're smarter than the police, and they are for a while until we catch on to their tricks. Then, we'll find them." She wrote something on her pad, then continued, "I'll see you two at 11:00 am."

We had forty-five minutes before our meeting. I couldn't keep still. Excitement built as the seconds ticked away until I could share our information.

Jo stepped away and returned, holding papers. She waved them in the air as she stated, "At your request, Ryker. The backgrounds for Mr. Priestly and Conner Piston."

Chapter 9

Jo planted the backgrounds on my desk, and as I watched her eyes, I made myself turn away before they did that thing. Too much was riding on today's meeting, and I couldn't afford to lose my train of thought.

Mr. Priestly's background rested on top, so I started with him. I didn't expect to find anything, but detectives must follow every lead. Mr. Priestly has never had a run-in with the law, not even a speeding ticket. That says something about a person. He's a rule follower. Next, I thumbed through his financials over the past ten years, and nothing jumped at me. It appears he lives below his means, and he lives alone in a modest house in Ft. Worth. Not finding anything there, I placed Mr. Priestly's file to the side.

Next in line was Conner Piston. He owns the security company with the red and yellow logo, and he purchased Mr. Priestly's company several years ago. Conner has multiple speeding tickets from across Texas. Since it didn't shock me, I moved on to his financials. I paused. His finances are borderline in the red. His business struggles and is up and down. Conner's credit is mediocre at best. His bank statement shows many trips to different cities in Texas, and again, he lives in Ft. Worth. Conner is divorced and without children.

Once I perused the backgrounds, Jo offered her opinion. "From what I've seen, Mr. Priestly is in the clear, but Conner is a different story. He fits with your profile. What are your thoughts?"

"I agree with you. How do you feel about a face to face meeting with Conner?" I asked with my eyebrow lifted and a grin on my face.

"I'd love to," Jo said, matching my grin.

"Since our meeting begins shortly, we'll contact Conner afterward." My pen glided across the page, and I noted another reminder. This meeting will be fun. I can feel it.

Jo sat on one side of me while Greta on the other. Then Sanchez and Schiller joined us and took seats on the same side of the table. I logged into the video meeting and waited. Dallas joined first, followed by Austin, then Houston. Unfortunately, Houston's connection was spotty because of the stormy weather that moved in from the Gulf.

Detective Garcia stated, "sorry for the connection. This storm is brutal. We have a massive outage south of Houston, and we're hoping we don't lose ours next. No one knew this storm was packing such a punch."

"We'll make this quick as possible. We've learned a few things over the last day, and we wanted to share. First, the killer hacks into the victim's security system and turns it off for them before entering their premises. Then, the victim's company records appear the victims turned their systems off from inside the house and no one is the wiser." The group nods in astonishment, then they clap. Finally, they discuss the security company angle and agree to investigate security companies in their immediate area. Once I finished my spiel, I turned it over to Jo to showcase her worksheet.

Jo passes a copy to Greta, Sanchez, and Schiller, explaining the worksheet to the team. I turn silent. This worksheet shakes me to my core. Jo notices my expression. "What's wrong, Ryker?"

"Can you all give me a minute?" I asked the group then my attention returned to Jo's sheet.

I felt Greta staring holes in my chest. Just as she opened her mouth to speak, I explained my actions. "Jo's worksheet gave us another clue. Everyone look at your sheet." I waited a minute for everyone to access their email. "Check the day of death column against the street number column. The killer selects the street number by the calendar date or vice versa. We know something happened to him in July and November, but I don't know the trigger yet, for the dates of death and the address." I paused. "This killer is intelligent. Maybe even off the charts."

Jo and Greta's mouths hung open. I leaned over, "you can close your mouth now. It's over."

The ladies fidgeted in their chairs, then looked at me. "Jo, this was brilliant. Without this, I'm unsure if anyone would have picked up on the correlation." I smiled at her then faced the group.

"I need you all to do two things before we talk again. First, check your addresses where the murders occurred in your area, and let me know if they fall within a distinct geographic area. Second, shift your concentration to security companies. If someone seems odd, bring them in for questions. If you need us, let us know." With that, we signed off.

Greta leaned back in her chair. "Great work. Let's follow Ryker's lead and pinpoint the crime scenes. He might be onto something." She stood and gave me a slight smile as she exited the room.

Jo stood and walked to a Ft. Worth street map. With her list in hand, she jabbed push pins into the crime scene addresses. A picture formed. The addresses from our crime scenes were within five miles of each other, except July 4, 2015, and that one was on the outskirts of town in lake country.

Schiller spoke, "that's amazing, Bartley. How did you know the scenes were so close together?"

"I didn't, really. It was a guess. But when I saw the correlation between the street numbers and the dates of death, I thought he might keep his killing zone local." I shared. "The closer the proximity, the easier it would be to keep track. When we find this guy, he'll have a notebook or a computer spreadsheet detailing his murders. This guy will be proud of his handiwork."

Everyone shook their head in disgust. How can someone go about killing people for ten years and not get caught?

"Oh, one more thing, Jo and I will meet with Conner Piston this afternoon if he's available. He owns the security company with the red and yellow logo. Look up some other companies and start your investigations with them."

The guys understood and agreed. They picked their gear up from the table and left the office, discussing the recent news. I listened to them as they walked away, realizing they had no idea of my capabilities. That's when I chuckled.

I stood and walked over to my desk. Thumbing through my notes from Mr. Priestly, I found Conner's number. I dialed it from my cell phone because I didn't want to spook him when the number registered as Ft. Worth Police Department.

Conner answered on the second ring. After I introduced myself, I explained my call. Conner asked, "what does this have to do with me?"

That's the same question all suspects ask. And we give the same answer. "We'll discuss that when we meet. Are you available at 2:30 today? We can meet at your office, or you can come to police headquarters, whichever works best for you."

Conner stammered, then finally agreed to meet us at his office. I gave a thumb up to Jo. She relaxed and straightened her desk. When I ended the call, Jo asked, "are you hungry? Because I'm starving."

"Of course, I'm hungry. I never skip a meal intentionally." We left the office searching for food, and neither wanted to eat at the food truck. We wanted a sit-down meal, and that's what we did. I drove to our favorite Mexican restaurant. Jo gave me a grin.

As it turned out, lunch was delicious as always and just what we needed. We talked about anything but the case. Madge's name entered the conversation about the middle way, and I flinched. Another day slipped by without her name entering my mind. What kind of husband am I? I should track her down, forcing her to talk to me. Does she have someone else in her life than she'd rather be with, because if she does, now is a good time to share?

"I'm sorry, Ryker. I shouldn't have mentioned Madge. That's between you two." Jo lowered her head and moved food around on her plate.

"Jo, I don't know what to say about Madge. Other than I feel like a failure as a husband because my wife doesn't enter my mind until someone else brings her name into our conversation. I'm pretty sure that's not how a marriage should be. I've asked myself a thousand times if I thought Madge had another guy in her life, but to be honest, I don't have a clue. She spends so much time at the hospital, I don't see how she could fit him into her life." Then Jo raised her eyes to mine.

"You are not a failure at anything. It takes two people to have a relationship. Everyone knows that. I'm just sorry Madge can't see that for your sake. But for my sake, not so much. My promise to you is I won't bring the subject up again. Let me know when the time is right. I'm not going anywhere." Jo grinned, and her eyes did that thing again.

I flinched because things changed for me sitting across the table from my partner. Maybe that's the sign, partner, not only work partner but could we make it as life partners? Of course, we'd have to live in secret because I'd bet Greta would ship one of us to another division, and neither of us wants that. That's the one troublesome issue.

Jo watched me squirm as crazy thoughts raced through my mind. Finally, she leaned over, placed her hand on mine, and said, "finish your lunch, Ryker. Our meeting with Conner is in forty-five minutes."

So, I did just that. As I swallowed the last bite of the largest burrito known to man, I wished I hadn't. It sits in my belly like a bowling ball. Before we left, our server gladly poured our sweet tea into

Styrofoam cups. Now, I'd have something to occupy my hands on the drive to Conner's. Even though I'd rather be holding Jo's hand.

At 2:25 pm, we entered Conner's business offices. He displayed his red and yellow logo on the entrance wall. When I saw it, a thought came to mind. Why would he target his own clients? That seems counterproductive from a business perspective. I glanced at Jo and realized I had an idea.

A young guy greeted us as we entered the office. He politely told us that Conner was on a business call and would notify us when Conner was available. After he stood from his chair, he pointed to a coffee bar in the corner. While I wanted a cup, we never accept drinks or food from potential suspects. It makes the police look weak. We learned that in police school 101. It's all about perception to the public.

I nudged Jo to the corner so I could share my thought. When I did, she tilted her head, then shrugged her shoulders. "That is a good question. So, are we following the wrong lead?"

"Not exactly. But I think the killer might be from a company that's doesn't have a security system for our victims." I tried to explain, but Jo didn't follow.

"I'm confused." Jo stated.

So, I tried again. "Think about it like this. If you own a security company, why would you target your own customers? If word circulated about the deaths of people with your system, wouldn't people think twice about signing up for your alarm service?" As I finished, I saw Jo's face lighten, and her face broke out into a grin.

"I get it now. You think the killer owns a company we know nothing about. So, the businesses in the victim's photo are exempt from our investigation, right?" Jo asked with an eyebrow lifted.

"They are not exempt but less likely to be our killer. Although, Conner sure fits the profile. Let's see what he has to say." I glanced at the clock on my cell phone. Ten minutes late, that doesn't bode well for him. We sit side by side and stare at the guy behind the desk as he answers calls and refers them to someone else.

At 2:55pm, Conner emerged from a door to our left. He wore khakis with a navy polo shirt sporting his logo. As he walked to greet us, he spouted an apology. When Conner saw Jo, he gravitated to her. Was it the lipstick? Or did he feel a connection? Either way, I didn't like it, and I tried to keep it to myself, but Jo noticed something in my demeanor.

Conner led us to his corner office. His office offered impressive views of downtown Ft. Worth. I laid my book on the table and jumped into questions. Conner provided alibis for the dates of the murders, which I half expected. While he played cool, he had a tough time keeping the sweat from his upper lip. So, I dug and pushed deeper and harder than I needed. When I explained our thoughts on computer hacking, Conner raised his eyebrows.

"You think someone hacked into my security company's computer system to turn off alarms with the sole intent of committing murder. That's unbelievable." Conner sat still as he contemplated my idea. Does he know something he isn't telling us? "Is that possible, Detectives?"

Jo answered, "We think so. That's why we're here. Several of your clients are our murder victims. We suspect you didn't kill them, but they had your security systems installed in their residences at the time of their deaths."

I took over the questions again. "Are any of your employees angry at you? Do you know anyone with computer skills that can hack into another company?" Then we waited while Conner tried to point us in another direction.

"No to all of your questions. I can ask my IT employees if they know how to trace a hack, but if they can't, I have a college friend that's always been into computers. He might help us."

"Call us back once you've spoken with your employees and your friend. Thanks for meeting us, Conner."

I stood and reached my hand for a shake. He obliged, then he turned to Jo and reached for her hand. As he shook it, I noticed his thumb stroked the top of her hand.

As we climbed into the car, Jo glanced at me across the roof, "what was all that about, Ryker? Were you mad he paid attention to me?" Jo sat in the seat and waited for an answer.

I paused long enough that I hoped Jo would forget her question. But it didn't work. "Ryker, talk to me."

"I guess. I can't explain why that guy got under my skin. You have strikingly good looks, and I shouldn't be mad at another guy making eyes at you. They'd be a fool not to." When I said it, I flinched because I said it out loud and to Jo.

"Really, Ryker? You mean what you said?" Jo countered in a pleading tone.

"Yes, Jo. I mean it. But I just don't know how to handle it yet." As I started the car sweat rolled down my back. Then I slammed into reverse and drove us back to the office. Neither felt like talking, or we didn't know what to say, but either way, it was quiet.

We didn't make it back until after five. I dropped Jo at her car and headed to the gym. I needed to think, and the gym was the best place I know to think.

Between the case, Madge, and Jo, I had a lot of thinking to do.

I worked through the case while I pounded out several miles on the treadmill. Tomorrow, I'd have the team refocus on security companies not mentioned in the crime scenes. From the treadmill, I moved to weights. Here is where Madge and Jo battled for time. It's time for Madge and me to decide our future. If she wants a husband, she needs to prove it. If not, we separate now. She can keep the house if she wants, or we can sell it and split our proceeds. Either way is fine for me. Then, Jo. What do I do with her? We have mutual feelings, that's obvious. But are we jeopardizing our careers? That's a question I can't answer by myself.

Rain began coming down in buckets while I spent time in the gym. The parking lot had puddles to my ankles that I tried to dodge as I ran to my car. As I slid into the car, I realized it didn't matter if I avoided the puddles or not. The rain soaked me to the bones. The water carried a chill to it, reminding me fall came in next week, as does college football. I grinned.

It took longer than usual to make my way home because of the weather. When it rains faster than your windshield wipers, that makes for a slow trip. As I pressed the button for the garage door, I wondered if Madge would greet me. That answer came quickly with a resounding no since the garage sat empty.

I shivered as I entered the house, and I wondered why. For some reason, I felt like something wasn't right, but I couldn't put my finger on it. After a quick perimeter check, I jumped into a scalding shower and let the water work on my shoulders. Once the tension eased, I dressed and headed downstairs for food and coffee since I missed my afternoon coffee break.

The television helped pass my time since college football shows started their previews. This time of year held the greatest of all sports, college football. There's nothing like the thrill of sitting in a stadium with a hundred thousand of your closest friends.

Overnight, rain poured from the heavens in buckets, and the wind drove it into my windows, but I finally slept. The case nor the girls kept me awake, and I felt like a new person. Except for the other side of the bed lay empty. The sheets were not touched, so Madge never made it home again. I guess the weather kept her busy.

As I reversed out of the garage, I noticed the gutter was full of running water. That means we've had enough rain, and flash floods would happen soon. Certain areas of our town are prone to flash floods, which always cause issues for the city.

The trip to the office was slow between rain and traffic. Jo beat me in today, but I still made it before she dried off. When I walked in, she had just hung her coat to dry. Then she giggled when she saw me. "No raincoat, Ryker?"

I glanced down and rain soaked me from head to toe. I shook my head like a dog, and water flew in all directions. Jo jumped back as I sprayed her. "I don't need another soaking," Jo exclaimed.

We spent a few minutes discussing Conner's meeting. Jo thinks he's hiding something, and I agree. But neither of us knew what. "Maybe he'll find someone to help us with the hacking. I'm 50/50 on him being the killer. He might work with an accomplice to handle the killings."

Jo stared at me as she shook her head. "You want him to be our killer. Ryker, that's so unlike you. You never make statements like that until you have evidence. You have none on Conner."

I nodded because Jo was right. We have no evidence pointing to Conner other than he owns a security company and fits my profile. But I'm sure there are others out there that do too. Greta called us from her office. She's waiting for an update.

We entered Greta's office, holding our coffee cups. Greta enjoys her coffee too. "I need an update. What have you learned?"

Over the next hour, we discussed our thoughts and our meeting with Conner. When she told us to let her know the outcome, my phone rang. I didn't recognize the number, so I silenced the call. Seconds later, the same number called again. This time, I answered, and my world shattered as I listened to a doctor from Madge's hospital tell me to meet him in her hospital room as soon as possible.

My co-workers knew something horrific had happened, but they waited patiently for me to absorb the news. "Madge is in the hospital. Her doctor requested me to join him. I'll call you both when I know more."

I bolted from the room, leaving my coffee cup on Greta's desk. What could have happened to her? Now, I felt guilty for not texting her when I made it home last night. The weather was so bad, I assumed she worked late. So much for assuming.

With the pouring rain, I took it slow. There wasn't any reason to cause an accident. The information desk pointed to the ICU on the third floor. I followed the green line on the floor and the walls marking my way. A doctor stood outside of Madge's door. I peeked into the room and noticed he had hooked Madge to every conceivable machine. Then I looked at the doctor in the eyes. They told me everything I needed to know.

"Detective Bartley, I'm Doctor Abel. I work with Madge, and I asked the police officers that found her to let me handle your contact. I hope that's okay. Patrol officers found Madge's vehicle in the woods on the side of a street. I'm assuming she was traveling home since we worked into the wee hours of the morning. She was unconscious when they found her. Detective, she's in a coma. We've scheduled tests to try to determine the extent of the coma." The doctor took a break for the news to sink into my brain.

"Are you saying she may never wake?" My eyes met his for a few seconds before he offered an answer.

"Yes. She may never wake, and if she does, she may never be the same. No one knows how long she laid in the car without treatment. The patrol officers found her at seven this morning when they started their patrols. The last I saw her at the hospital was 3:00 am. That's a long time."

I didn't know what to say or do. Finally, Doctor Abel opened Madge's room door for me to enter, but I didn't know if I could. I've experienced nothing like this before. When the hospital called me for Jo, she could speak. This time, Madge can't talk. She has a ventilator in her mouth, IVs hung to one side, and all kinds of monitors beeped and gurgled.

Inch by inch, I made my way to her side. I laid my hand on her arm, and I stroked it. Doctor Abel suggested I speak with her. If she hears you, she might squeeze your hand. It was worth a try. So I followed his instructions, but nothing happened.

Her eyelids never moved, nor did her hands. I was at a loss.

When nurses entered her room, I left. I couldn't watch that. I called Greta and then Jo. Jo had tears and said she would see me later. Greta asked me about the case, and I told her I still wanted it. I couldn't do anything for Madge in her condition, but I would have to make trips to the hospital. Then, I thought about her parents. I must call them and hear the questions that I can't answer.

Before Jo made it to the hospital, I did what husbands are supposed to do, and I called Madge's parents. Her mom broke down, but her dad played strong. I liked her dad. After I gave them hospital instructions, I asked her dad to text me when they arrived.

I paced the ICU waiting room for what felt like hours. The accident still made me feel guilty, but I know it shouldn't. At three in the morning, I had been asleep for hours, so even if I sent her a text, it would have been hours before. I don't know why I felt the need to relieve myself of guilt, but I did. When I heard the door open, I turned, and Jo stood in the doorway.

We walked to each other and wrapped each other in a hug. I needed it more than she knew. When we separated, I told her everything. I knew tears had flowed down her face because it left red-rimmed eyes behind. But Jo still sported the hot pink

lipstick. We sat side by side when Doctor Abel
entered the room. He walked over to us, and I gave
him permission to talk freely in front of Jo.

"Madge is on her way to get a CAT scan. It will be
several hours before you can see her." Then he
turned to Jo. "Make him eat lunch. Sitting here will
cause the strongest to crumble." He patted us each
on the knee then he left.

Jo glanced at me. "Let's go, Ryker. We'll eat then
discuss the case. That will help pass the time."

We wandered down to the hospital cafeteria. It must
have good food because people packed it. There
were several items from which to choose. I
purchased a chicken sandwich while Jo picked a
fruit bowl. Neither of us felt like eating, but the
doctor was right.

Jo brought up the case, and we discussed our next
moves. She jotted notes on a white paper napkin
since she'll handle the case today. I need to be here
for Madge's parents.

Chapter 10

As I waited for the elevator, Jo touched my arm and then reached up and hugged me. I didn't want to let go, but we each had pressing things to handle today. She promised to call me later. I watched her walk out the front door, and the elevator doors closed.

There were no changes to Madge's condition while we were away, so I plopped down in the chair next to her bed. Since I wasn't sure what to do, I stared out the window because I couldn't bear to see Madge in that bed. That's not Madge. She's brilliant, and medicine is everything to her. That's her true calling. I should have seen it earlier. We love each other, but there isn't enough time in a day to prove it, not with our jobs competing for the same amount of time.

The minutes ticked by with no activity. My mind wandered to Jo and the team. We made great strides in finding this guy when the hacking topic came out. That explains how the killer makes entry, but it doesn't tell us the killer's identity. Jo will have a full afternoon with the calls. I'm excited to hear the results.

By late afternoon, the nurses checked on Madge every so often. They offered no encouraging words. They merely typed numbers into the computer, smiled at me, then closed the door on their way out.

It was close to 6:00 pm before Madge's parents arrived. A nurse escorted them to Madge's room. Both parents hugged me before they walked to their daughter's side.

They spent several minutes with her before turning back to me. I had taken up space by the window. We chatted softly about Madge and the accident. No one could explain the cause of the accident. The police blamed the weather. For me, I think Madge fell asleep at the wheel, but I would never tell her parents that. If they must bury their only daughter, there is no reason to place blame on Madge.

I reminded Madge's parents of the CAT scan, and we should hear the results tomorrow. Then, I passed them a house key and told them they were free to stay the night at our house. They can come and go as they please. Madge's mom cried, and her dad shook my hand.

A nurse entered while we stood around Madge's bed. I took that moment to escape with the excuse of work. With my phone in my hand, I'm hoping they assumed I have a work-related call. Once I cleared the ICU, I bolted down the stairs. I needed air.

When I walked outside, I gulped air. That's when I noticed the air turned cooler after the soaking rains. It felt nice. Clouds remained in the sky, not willing to let go of their hold. I texted Jo that I left the hospital and was heading to the gym and would like to hear her afternoon events because I expected great news.

The gym time was precisely what I needed to settle my anxiety. By the time I made it home, I felt somewhat normal. After my shower, I texted Jo. Within seconds, my phone rang. Once we cleared the pleasantries and Madge's update, we jumped into the case.

"Sit back, Ryker. I have several updates. First, Detective Jones called, and they have several companies that require a deeper dive into their backgrounds. He'll call back tomorrow to discuss their findings. Then, Conner called, and his IT workers are not into hacking or didn't admit it if they could hack a computer system. Conner called his college friend, Erik Cleggman, who lives in Dallas. He wasn't available, so Conner will call when he hears from Erik." Jo paused for air. I kept my questions until later.

Jo continued her updates. "Greta gave me the name of a guy in the crime lab who is part of the cyber-crime unit. His name is Lyle Ashwell, and he knows hacking. I covered the preliminaries this afternoon, and he agreed with your idea. So we're meeting in the morning. Lyle will work with Conner, and if Lyle can trace Conner's hacking issue, we might find our killer."

The amount of work covered in one afternoon impressed me. "Jo, you all did great today. Sounds like we are moving forward. Thanks for the call. I'll call tomorrow." I ended the call because Madge's dad called me on the other line.

When I returned his call, he just wanted me to know they would be home around midnight. A sigh of relief escaped my lips because I dreaded the call. With the new case information, I went to bed for sleep, but dreams fought me every step of the way. When the doorknob rattled, I expected Madge to enter our room shortly afterward. When she didn't, another dream took her place.

Morning came with the sky still dark. I sat up on the bed's side and rested my elbows on my legs. What was becoming of my life? It's strange not knowing what the next phone call would bring. Today, we find out Madge's CAT scan results. I feel I already know the answer, but I guess I need to hear it. Until then, I'm going to the office.

I showered and dressed quickly, then I sent Jo a text letting her know I'd meet her at the office. She called. "Ryker, there's no need for you to come to the office. You need to be with Madge."

"There's nothing I can do there. Her parents are with her. When the results of the scan are ready, I'll be there for the results." No one could keep me from the office. I needed to think about anything but Madge.

On my drive to the office, I grabbed two dozen donuts. That should hold my group for ten minutes, then I chuckled as I scarfed one down in less than ten seconds.

Greta and I walked into the office together. I surprised her because she thought I would be at the hospital too. Just as I placed the donuts on the counter, Jo entered with a fresh shirt and red lipstick. I smiled.

While Greta and I stood at the counter waiting for the coffee, Jo told us of her call last night. "Conner called last night. His friend, Erik from Dallas, is in town today, and they will meet me here at the office."

Jo saw the look I gave her but said nothing because Greta stood between us. Then Greta said, "Jo if Ryker isn't available, grab Sanchez or Schiller to join you in the meeting. I know it's here, but safety first since we're unsure of the killer's identity."

"Will do, Greta. We set the meeting for ten. Lyle already started working on Conner's hacking job. It might take a day before he has any evidence. I haven't heard from Detective Cabello on the Dallas companies yet. Houston and Austin joined forces yesterday since several of their companies overlap."

Greta thanked Jo for handling the case yesterday, and then she told me to do whatever I needed to for Madge. I nodded.

Jo and I ambled off to our room. "Why didn't you mention to me about your meeting with Conner and Erik last night?" I asked of Jo with a hint of concern.

"I didn't know it when we talked. Conner called me later, and we set the time then. It's no big deal. I wanted to meet Erik and see if he could help with the hacking aspect, but it sounds like Lyle might have it handled for us. I can cancel the meeting if you think it's best." Jo offered.

Ryker ponders the meeting with Conner and moves forward with it. Not sure why but something tells him to meet these guys. So, they discuss questions for Erik about hacking and how computer savvy he might be.

Detective Jones calls Ryker, "I am so sorry to hear about Madge. We're praying for you both."

"Thanks, Jones. I appreciate your sentiment."

"I also need to update you on our security companies. We are down to two companies that we are investigating, and both owners fit your profile. We had three companies until we found out one company is owned by a 5'4" woman who weighs a whopping 90 lbs."

Jo and I chuckled as there was no way she could garrote a grown man without a fight.

"Sounds like you're on the right path. Let us know what you find. Thanks for the update, Jones."

I glanced at my desk and spotted the two untouched cases from Plano and Wichita Falls. Plano sat on top, so I began with that one. In Plano, on Sunday, July 10, 2016, someone suffocated a lady while she laid on her sofa watching television. The victim moved to town twenty-one days prior for a new job. She rented the condo. The collected evidence was a torn piece of a receipt, and someone ripped a page from her day timer for the date of death. When the victim didn't show for work, her new manager grew concerned and called the police. The responding officers saw her body through a window from the back deck. No one noted if there was a security system at her residence.

"Jo, here's the file on the Plano murder. I'm starting on Wichita Falls next." When I glanced at Jo, she was nodding to me with her hand out for the file.

Wichita Falls joined the serial killer murders on Thursday, November 9, 2017. This one churned in my belly. The killer used a garrote to murder a couple, just like the Rivera's. I immediately went to the photos. A window decal showing a red, white and blue logo stared back at me. Why is it the same company? Is someone targeting the company?

Then, I read the evidence report, which offered little. The scene description was eerily similar to the Rivera's too. The killer murdered the man in his office, followed by his wife in the kitchen. The couple has grown kids, and one is a doctor at the downtown hospital. He couldn't reach his dad, so he drove to the house on Friday around noon. He found and identified the bodies.

It appears the man fought the attacker because he placed his index finger under the garrote, but the killer overpowered him, cutting his fingertip off before killing him.

The crime scene found blood on the desk's corner with a smeared palm print in it.

I closed this file, and ideas floated around my mind. Jo finished the first file and cleared her throat with her hand in the air, waiting for the second file. "Read this one closely, then we'll talk," I suggested.

Jo's eyebrows grew together, "yes, sir." I passed the file to her, and while she read it, I pondered ideas.

Since I kept reading the same security company names, I wanted to know if they were the target. Is the killer trying to steer business away from these companies? When the public hears that a security system doesn't prevent a murder, they would be less likely to do business with them.

Detective Jones texted me and stated that one of his business owners will be at the office at 2:00pm, but the other is out of town. So, he'll schedule that meeting as soon as he returns.

Jo finished reading the Wichita Falls case when she faced me. "This one was brutal, Ryker. The killer learned his craft over the years. There's no other murder with missing fingertips."

"Agree. But that's not my concern. I've noticed the residences have some of the same security companies. Are the companies targets too? Is the killer trying to discredit the companies at our murder victim's homes?"

"Wichita Falls had a red, white and blue decal which was Priestly. Conner bought Priestly. Has Conner made enemies in his business? But wait, Plano had no sticker and no system that we're aware of, anyway."

I grinned when I said, "she might have been looking for a security system, and she chose the wrong one. In the Plano file, they mention a missing page from her day timer. She might have had someone stop in for a quote. Now I wonder if they still hold the day timer in evidence. If so, I want it."

Jo's desk phone rang. She grabbed it and listened. As she placed the phone into the cradle, she stood. "Our guys are here."

I grabbed a pen and my notebook. This meeting will prove interesting. I followed Jo to the lobby to meet the guys. Conner placed his hand on Jo's arm while Erik stood back and watched the show. It's obvious Conner likes Jo. Both men dressed in khakis and polo-style shirts. Conner's boasted his logo on the left side while Erik's was plain.

When we entered the interview room, the men sat across from us. Erik spoke little until I started with questions about computers. He admitted to working with computers most of his life. While he isn't a hacker by trade, he could trace a hack. Erik asked to meet with Lyle and offered his services. Anything to get the police to leave Conner alone.

Erik confirmed Conner's story about their meeting in college. After they left the University, Conner moved to Ft. Worth, and Erik returned to Dallas. They still see each other often. Both are divorced, and neither have kids. Could these guys be partners in these murders?

Before I could gather my thoughts on that, Jo called Lyle and agreed to meet Erik. He's on his way to meet us. Conner chatted with Jo during our wait, but I couldn't hear his question. Instead, a smile spread across Erik's face, so I assume he heard it.

A knock sounded from our door. I opened it to see Lyle carrying his laptop. He had a strange look on his face but said nothing. He entered, and Jo introduced him to our guests. I slid my chair over to the side so Lyle could sit closer to Erik. Lyle shared where he was with the hack job, and Erik's eyebrows drew together, and then his eyebrows lifted, as if in surprise, then a slight facial tick appeared next to his mouth. From my spot in the room's corner, I watched both shows. Conner trying to get Jo to agree to supper, and Lyle holding back on what he shared with Erik.

I jotted a reminder to contact Lyle. He had the information that I needed. Lyle and Erik spoke for fifteen minutes, exchanging contact information, then Lyle left us for his office meeting. Jo escorted the guys to the door, and I headed for my desk. That was an odd meeting. I called Lyle and left a message for him to contact me.

Jo returned to the office, and she carried a strange expression on her face. "Everything okay?" I inquired.

"I suppose. Conner is relentless. He doesn't take no for an answer."

I didn't answer because my text message sounded. Madge's parents request my presence at the hospital. "I've got to run to the hospital. I'll call later if I don't return."

When I climbed into my car, I took a minute to steady myself. I wasn't sure how I was supposed to feel with a partner I think I loved and a wife in a coma. How did I let my life come to this?

I braced for whatever news came my way. If Madge survived, I'd be grateful. Just because our marriage wasn't the greatest, I didn't want her to die.

Madge's parents greeted me at the waiting room door.

"Ryker, the news isn't good." Madge's dad spoke. "The CAT scan revealed no brain activity. They took her back for surgery. I think they called it a craniectomy and decompression surgery or something close. We are so emotional we can't remember all these technical terms. They took her back fifteen minutes ago."

"Are they giving us any hope she'll wake after these procedures?" I questioned since I didn't have time to meet the doctor before surgery.

Madge's mom gave me hope, but her dad's eyes told me another story. One that I feared from the moment I saw her in the hospital bed. I nodded because words wouldn't come.

I sat next to the wall and laid my head over. My head felt heavy, and it took too much effort to hold it upright. While I waited, I worked on the case. I rehashed the meeting from beginning to end. Something was off, but I couldn't explain it.

As I dosed, Lyle called. I answered as I walked away from Madge's parents. We discussed the meeting, and Erik bothers Lyle more than Conner. He agreed both guys were similar in their actions. Lyle confirmed Erik knows computers as Erik showed Lyle an easier way to handle a problem. Then Lyle said, "I'm confused why Erik pointed out the new way. It's like he tried to bypass a whole coded string in the hacking job. So, I'll compare Erik's way versus mine. When I'm satisfied, I'll let you know."

"Thanks, Lyle." Why would one computer person try to divert someone's attention? Is Erik hiding something? I want a background check on Erik. I texted Jo with the request. She replied with a question mark. Then I got mad. Is she covering for these guys?

After taking a deep breath, I resent the request. She replied with an ok, and she didn't know I was returning to the office today, no matter how late. I'm eager to read the report on Erik because it might be just what we needed.

Two hours later, Madge's doctor walks into the room. Both procedures went off without a hitch, but the wait is on again. He said we might not see improvement for twenty-four hours. It hit me when he looked me in the eye. The surgery was at her parent's request, not his. Madge wasn't coming home. It was time I accepted it. I told everyone I was returning to work for a few hours, but I'd return. Madge's mom gave me a strange look, but her dad nodded. I took that as acceptance.

I drove to the office in a stupor because I was unsure what I should think or do. How many husbands bolt from the hospital where their wives lay in a coma? I've had enough experiences with death to know you can't change some outcomes. So there's no need to dwell on it.

By the time I made it back, the parking lot had sat empty. Either the detectives were out working a case, or everyone went home. Jo's car wasn't in the lot either. Maybe she ran the report and left it for me. I ran up the stairs instead of taking the elevators, and it winded me, and that was a shock.

I glanced around the office, then I walked to my desk. When I found no background report, I wandered into our temporary office. Jo didn't run the background check on Erik. Why?

While I sat at my desk jotting notes for tomorrow, Jo called my cellphone. I answered and waited. "I didn't think you'd answer, so I waited for voicemail to answer. How are things, Ryker?"

I gave Jo the rundown on Madge. The entire story and more. I confessed to not knowing how I was supposed to feel or act. It's as if I'm in a bubble. She listened, just like always. We discussed Madge's accident, which reminded me to get the police report since I haven't read it yet.

Jo moved on to the case, and she gave me the update on Houston and Austin with zip. They claim to be a bust with their business owners. All three had alibis for the dates of death. Then she stated Detective Jones didn't call back after his meeting. We agreed he was waiting until he spoke to both owners. Jo promises to run the background check tomorrow morning, as she didn't realize I would return tonight.

After Jo's call, I dialed Detective Cabello. I needed to pacify my curiosity. He and Jones just wrapped an interview. This guy was older than they first thought. He also had an alibi for the murder. The guy also admitted to not traveling as much as he did when he first began his business. Jones had one more interview in the morning. He'll call once that's over.

I left the office and headed back to the hospital. I called Madge's dad and offered to bring them food. He gladly accepted. We ate in silence in the waiting room. I visited Madge during permitted times, but I saw no change, just more bandages around her head. Fluid drained through the tubes, but I saw no hope, and I had no one to share it with. I didn't want to be the one to tell her mom, but somehow, I think her dad knows.

At ten, I left to go home. Madge's parents would come later. While we sat in the waiting room, there wasn't much to talk about. I had hoped they would ask about Madge and what I wanted to do about her health because I feared the doctor would approach us any day and ask us to make the heart-wrenching decision to leave her hooked up forever or pull the plug. I cringed.

I was the first arrival at the office because I couldn't face Madge's parents this morning. The hospital gave me the bleak news of no change overnight, so I went to work. I pulled Jo's worksheet and studied it again. I worked on finding the correlation between the weekday, date of death, and the street number of the victims. Does the killer choose the date of death first or the street number? Is the street number selected randomly, or is it familiar with the victim?

If the security companies with the yellow and green logo went out of business, that leaves Conner's business the only one left from our list. Is that a clue? Is someone targeting Conner's business?

Jo and Greta entered the office together and walked to my desk. They asked for an update, and Greta told me to go to the hospital. When I explained why I couldn't, she understood and moved to the coffee bar while Jo stared at me. She knows I'm conflicted.

Just as she opened her mouth, my desk phone rang. I watched her hang her coat across the back of her chair as the crime lab called with the best news in a while. They matched two fibers, and they guessed they're from a Ford van or pickup truck. They'll have confirmation in an hour. The lab tech knew I wanted information yesterday. "So, our guy drives a Ford. It could be a van or pickup truck. Didn't one report mention a van?"

Jo thumbed through the reports and found it. "November 6, 2018, murder has the mention of a flower delivery van at the house two days before the murder. Did we see flowers in the pictures? Then in July 2014, a neighbor reported seeing a white van but then retracted her statement."

"Pull the pictures of the November 2018 murder. Let's confirm the flower delivery. But I suspect our guy drives a Ford van or pickup truck. I suspect it would have a logo, but could he change it?"

"Maybe he doesn't need to change it. Were these victims in the market for a new security alarm company? He could have scoped out the house while he discussed his services. If they told him no, he killed them." Jo suggested with a head tilt and shoulder shrug.

I didn't give her a reply as her questions rolled around in my head. Picking her worksheet back off the desk, I studied it again but with a fresh perspective. I agreed it's possible the killer had the address before the date of death. The killer visits an address for a quote, the victim refuses his service, he plans their end. It works.

Jo still stared at me after I worked through the scenario. I repeated my thoughts out loud to Jo, and I still liked the ending. She grinned and gave me a high five. We need to find out who these victims met with before their death.

Standing from my desk, I walked into our temp office. The evidence boxes sat against the wall. I would go through each one, hoping to find a calendar or a mention of an appointment. Jo sat at her desk, and as I walked through the doorway, she yelled, "I'll run Erik's background."

I didn't acknowledge it because we had a new plan. We now had the fibers matching a van or truck, and we knew how the killer chooses his victims. The question of why remains elusive.

Jo and I spent two hours combing through the evidence boxes, looking for calendars to prove our theory. One report stated a page from the victim's day timer was missing, presumably by the killer. We still had cellphones we could try to recover. All we need is a name. I called the crime lab for the tech working with the Rivera's cellphone. She stated the cellphones remained charged, and she'd look for us.

I noted the time was 11:00 am. Detective Jones and Cabello should be in a meeting with their last business owner. I hope something comes from this. If not, we wasted a lot of time.

We decided on an early lunch because I wanted to be available once Jones and Cabello finished their meeting. Neither of us spoke of Madge. While I thought of her often, I tried not to dwell on it.

Jo and I walked into the office at 12:15 pm, but I still hadn't heard from Jones. I contemplated calling him, but I refrained. We needed a meeting today in case things changed for me. I didn't want to leave the team hanging even though Jo could lead. I just didn't want to miss anything.

With the worksheet in my hands, Jo slid Erik's background check across my worksheet. I caught it before it hit the floor. "Anything good in it?" I asked as I skimmed the top half.

"Not really," Jo replied, but I heard a question in her voice.

I continued reading it. His name, date of birth, and address matched what he provided to us in our meeting. The background confirmed he attended college with Conner. He worked in the computer industry from college until now. Now, he owns his own business, Cleggman Enterprises. I raised my eyebrow when I read the name, then I glanced at Jo. She knew my question without asking it because she smiled as she passed another piece of paper my way.

"Cleggman Enterprises has several businesses that Erik runs as DBAs. One of which is an alarm security company in Dallas." My mind swirled with ideas. Then I swore to myself.

"Why didn't I ask him about his business while he sat across the table from us?" I ran my hands through the hair as tingles ran up my spine as a question entered my mind. Who is Detective Jones meeting today?

I snatched the phone from my desk and dialed Jones. When I got no answer, I dialed Cabella. He told me he missed the meeting this morning because of another case. Jones met with a guy, but he's at lunch. Cabella promised to have Jones return my call.

Chapter 11

Erik Cleggman could be our killer, and Jones met him alone. I don't like it, and I paced as I waited for Jones to call back. I had my cellphone in my hand to call him back when his contact information flashed on my home screen.

"Jones, thanks for calling. What's the name of the business owner you met today?"

I waited, and when he told me Erik Cleggman, I grinned at Jo. Then I asked about Erik's demeanor and the facial tic. Erik never mentioned to Jones that he met Jo and me at the office and discussed computers. After I gave Jones the back story on Erik, he went silent. Then he promised to take another look at the interview video and forward a copy to me because he didn't recall the facial tic. Erik will email documents to prove his alibis for the murders by tomorrow.

"Jones, with that guy's computer skills, he can make whatever receipt he wants." Jones chuckled and said he'd be available for the afternoon meeting.

Ten minutes later and we sat watching the interview between Jones and Erik. We noticed the facial tic, but we knew where to look for it. It only happened a few times when Jones mentioned street addresses.

Finally, Jo asked, "Is this our killer, or is he working with Conner?"

I didn't have the answer yet, but I will when the time comes to arrest the killer. When the video stopped, I clicked out of it and moved on to the DMV site. I wanted the DMV records for Conner and Erik. Once Conner's records were printed, I entered the same for Erik. When I had both records, I plucked them from the printer and laid them on my desk.

"Jo, not that this is a surprise, but both our guys drive Ford vehicles. They each own a Ford truck for personal use, and they have Ford trucks and vans registered to their businesses." I finished reading the reports then passed them to Jo. "Here you go."

She took them from my hand then read the reports. I heard a groan here and there, but nothing else. Jo had the same thoughts as me. One or both of these men is our killer. We just needed evidence to prove it.

The 2:00 pm meeting started on time with everyone in attendance. Commander Tiller began the meeting with a question about Erik Cleggman. So, we jumped into what information we had about Erik, including vehicles, computer knowledge, and he kept certain things away from Jones. Tiller didn't know that tidbit, and he pounced. Jo and I explained the circumstances of Erik's visit with us. While I spoke with the team, I sent Lyle a text asking him to join us.

After a few minutes of roundtable discussions, Lyle enters the room. I explained Lyle's presence and asked Lyle to explain what his comparison proved. "Hi everyone. At Ryker's request, I compared a coding string to a shortcut that Erik mentioned. When I tried to compare them, I noticed two things. First, when Erik pointed out a new way of tracking a hacker, his eagerness was awkward. Second, that afternoon I returned to the hacking software I've used for years, and someone changed the string. I don't have an explanation yet, but I will. If Erik is as good as he says, he might have jumped back into the hacking sequence and changed it before I could return to it."

Lyle paused, giving everyone time to absorb his thoughts. Then, Detective Schiller posed a question, "are you saying this guy hacked into your software program and changed the coding sequence, or did he hack into the original code and change it?"

Schiller impressed me with his question, and it caught Greta's attention too. "He didn't hack into our system, just the original code. Here's the good part. I saved the original coding string before I started working on it." Lyle explained with a grin. Then he continued, "I'm running another software program on it now. The answer is forthcoming. Once I have the IP address, I'll trace it to the hacker."

Everyone grinned as they leaned back in their chair. Then I took over, "Great work, Lyle. Now onto the physical evidence. The crime lab confirmed the fibers from several of our murders were from vehicle carpets. However, our issue is that we don't have evidence for a judge to sign a warrant for Erik and Conner's vehicle fibers. Another disheartening fact is the guys have purchased newer vehicles since the first murder in 2011. So we have nothing to compare those fibers to." I glanced at each team member as they thought of ways to secure the fibers without a warrant.

No ideas came to mind. Then Jo spoke, "we've contacted the crime lab for the Rivera's cell phones. We're looking for a calendar appointment for Erik or Conner's business. We suspect the killer meets with the victims for a business quote. If the victim decides against the quote, they become the next murder victim. It seems to me Conner isn't the killer because the victims mostly have his system installed in their residence."

Detective Jones raised his hand as he rehashed his interview with Erik and highlighted that Erik didn't share about his meeting with Jo and me. Everyone agreed that was by design. But Jones took the deception personal.

Once the meeting ended, Jo moved to social media. She wanted to see Erik and Conner's online presence. Jo motioned me to join her. She showed me both personal and business sites for each man. Jo had her work cut out for her. I left her to it.

My day ended as I drove to the hospital. This was my first visit of the day. I entered the waiting room to find Madge's parents sitting in the same chairs as the day before. I don't know how they do it. It would be understandable if they could sit next to Madge and hold her hand or something but sitting in this room would make me go insane.

Madge's mom saw me first, and she jumped up and ran to me with a grin as she told me Madge moved her hand. It shocked me to hear it, so I asked her to repeat it. "Ryker, Madge moved her hand. It wasn't much, but her thumb moved across the sheet."

"Has the doctor been in to meet with you since then?" I asked because I wanted to know of her chances of coming out of the coma or if the movement was merely muscle contractions.

Madge's dad responded, "we haven't seen the doctor" in a subdued tone, so he suspected the same as me while Madge's mom held onto a sliver of hope.

I checked the visitation schedule on the wall. "I'm going in for a visit." Turning, I walked out the waiting room door, and pushed the button on the wall for the nurse. She opened the door for me.

Madge laid in the same position as the doctors and nurses continued to pump medicine into her. The machines still did their job. I asked the nurse about the movement. She didn't want to answer me, so she said the doctor would explain everything. That told me what I needed to know. Madge's movement was muscle contractions. She wasn't waking.

I'd speak with the doctor, then I'd have a difficult conversation with Madge's parents. It's time to let her go if the doctors feel there is no chance of recovery. I'm not one to hang on to those that won't be back. I know Madge wouldn't want us to leave her like that. She is too vibrant a person and too smart to live on machines.

With it being late in the evening, I felt the doctor wouldn't make his rounds until tomorrow, and I'd be here with questions. I wanted the truth and all of it.

I split the visitation time with Madge's parents. When they came into the room, I went home, and I didn't stop at the gym. I couldn't bring myself to do it. Madge weighed heavy on my heart.

While I laid in bed watching a football game replay, Jo texted me. I called her back, and we talked about the case. She didn't ask about Madge because my mood told her everything. Jo mentioned Detective Jones has Erik in his crosshairs, and he planned on surveilling Erik tonight for a few hours. He wants to see what he does after work hours.

For an unknown reason, I sat up in bed. "Jo, I don't like that. Jones doesn't need to do this alone. Erik is sneaky. Isn't there someone that can help him?"

"The way Jones described it, he was only going to watch Erik for a few hours, nothing overnight."

I pondered the idea, then agreed. There wasn't anything I could do about Jones because he isn't mine, but Commander Tiller could. I'd talk with Jones tomorrow and then decide if I needed to involve Tiller.

Once our call ended, I flipped off the television and tried to sleep. Dreams of Madge flooded my mind. Our marriage was fun for a while, then life took over, and things changed. I still love her and always will.

When morning came, I called the hospital before I left the bed. There had been no change in Madge's condition overnight, and the doctor made his rounds around 8:30 am. I'd be there. I texted Jo about my hospital visit first, then I'd come to the office.

After a shower, I felt somewhat better but still somber because I knew what was coming, but I had prepared myself days ago. I just hope Madge's parents prepared themselves for the inevitable outcome.

On my drive to the hospital, I dialed Detective Jones, hoping he was awake. With his late hours last night, I might disturb his sleep. Jones answered on the second ring as he walked into his office. He described Erik's surveillance by saying Erik's night was just as dull as his. Erik went home after work and stayed there all night. The lights went out around midnight, and Jones left at 1:00 am.

Then I asked Jones about Erik's house. Jones continued by saying Erik lives in a moderately priced neighborhood. A pickup truck was parked in the garage, and he parked his work van in the drive. Erik walked to the mailbox and returned inside. A few downstairs lights were on for a while, then around 9:00 pm, he went upstairs and watched television or worked on a computer because a blue tint shone through the window.

While it disappointed me Erik did nothing of consequence, I'm glad Jones was safe. I expressed safety first and for him to take a partner if he watches Erik again. Jones asked a question, "do you think Erik locks his work truck at night?"

"I would think so, especially if it's loaded with equipment. So why are you asking?"

"We could grab some vehicle fibers from his van and see if they match. I know the results wouldn't be admissible in court, but we would know and could find a way to make it stick." Jones explained. I paused while I thought through the possible ramifications. "Let's sit on that idea for a couple of days. While I'd rather not do that, we might have too if we can't find enough evidence tying him to the murders."

When our call ended, I found myself in the hospital parking lot. I watched Madge's parents enter the lot and park two rows over from me. They entered the hospital before me, and we were already seated in the waiting room when I entered. We greeted one another but nothing more. Everyone expected the worst today.

At 8:35 am, Madge's doctor entered the waiting room. He didn't seem surprised to see us waiting. Before I let him speak, I asked about the hand movement. He confirmed my suspicion of a muscle contraction, but her mom refused to accept it. The doctor gave us a sliver of hope. He described the brain as receding but slower than usual. Against my better judgment, I agreed to one last test for Madge's mom. If it showed no change, we would remove Madge from life support. While Madge's dad accepted her fate, her mom never would.

Instead of the office, I returned home because this is something I've thought of several times over the last few days, but I refused to act on it. We have a lockbox tucked into a safe in our closet wall with our important papers tucked inside.

After we married, we wrote our last wishes on paper and placed them in a sealed envelope. While I was in the military, this was something our leader preached. Never leave your grieving family guessing. So, I needed to prepare myself to discuss Madge's wishes with her parents.

Madge's envelope held her doctor's script, and I grinned because it was something we joked about often. I slid my finger under the flap. Then, taking a deep breath, I read it as unshed tears teetered on the verge of spilling over the edge. After I finished reading it, I glanced outside and noticed the change in the weather. The leaves had color to them while others danced their way to the ground. How had I missed the change?

I moved to the bed and sat for a spell as I came to terms with Madge's death. My Madge. We had so many plans for our future. Sometimes life throws a curveball, and you must change your stance and correct your swing when it does. I should know this from my military days. Over the years, I've had to change my stance several times since I lost the military, then the guys I served with, and now Madge.

In the silence of our bedroom, I pondered the question, is it me? Am I the reason my life is full of death?

I glanced at the letter, returned it to the envelope, and laid it on the dresser. Now, I was ready to face Madge's parents with her desires in death. At least I had the letter, and they would know I spoke the truth.

With this in mind, I drove to work. I needed something else to occupy my time. Jo approached me first, and we stepped into our temporary office. I shared Madge's condition and my suspicion. She sympathized with me as a lone tear slid down her face.

I wanted to reach out and whisk the tear away for her, but I refrained. Instead, I looked to the door when Greta entered.

"Everything okay, Ryker?" she asked with a tinge of sadness.

I repeated my conversation with Jo, and Greta's eyes held tears too. Then, I asked about the case to change the subject because I couldn't discuss Madge anymore.

Jo cleared her throat, then offered, "the crime lab called about Rivera's phones. Mr. Rivera had a calendar appointment two days before the murders with someone with the initials ECE. If we can prove that's Erik, we have our evidence."

"ECE?" I repeated. Then it hit me, "Erik Cleggman Enterprises." I grinned.

"Did you speak with Jones?" Jo inquired.

I rehashed Jones' conversation with Jo and Greta. Greta wasn't fond of Jones surveilling Erik alone either. Greta will mention it to Commander Tiller in passing. While we didn't want to cause Jones any problems with his commander, we wanted him to know.

Lyle called my cell phone asking for a meeting, and I told him I was in the office with Greta and Jo. As he ended the call, he told me to hang tight. I'm guessing that's lingo for sit still.

Within sixty seconds, Lyle trotted into our office out of breath. "I took the stairs. You need to see this." Lyle placed his computer on the table in front of him. He clicked a few keys, then turned it to face us. It took me a minute to decipher the screen. Lyle had snapped a picture of a computer code and compared it with another code. They appeared one on top of the other. I saw it, but I didn't understand the significance.

Greta beat me to it. "What are we looking at here, Lyle? I get its computer coding, but why is it important?"

With a grin spreading from the side of his face to the other, he states, "someone hacked into Conner's system and changed the original code that Conner gave us."

"Why would they do that? Are they planning their next kill? We have a month before he kills again." I asked as I rubbed my hand through my hair.

Jo played with her earring, and Greta worked her jaws. We waited for the climax. "While I can't answer for the hacker, I can tell you he's trying to confuse me. He's sabotaging the software program I'm using to track him. In other words, he deleted a portion of the code and replaced it with a new string. So he thinks he's sending me someplace else when in fact, I have the original code."

Then I understood, "Erik, or the hacker if it's not Erik, thinks he can swing you away from him, but he can't because you were smart enough to copy the original code from Conner's computer. I wonder if Conner understood we suspect Erik hacks into his system for his targets. Is Erik hoping customers will leave Conner and join his security company?"

"That's it. I need a new security system. I'll have Conner and Erik give me quotes. Let's see what Erik does when I tell him no." Jo exclaimed while Greta and I shook our heads. There was no way I could let Jo do this.

"I see you both shaking your heads. Do you have another plan?" Jo asked, defeated.

"We'll get him. You playing as a decoy will be the last on my list." The thought of Jo fighting off a murderer sent shivers up my spine, even if she is a cop. I didn't want to put her in that spot.

Another thought crossed my mind. "Lyle, do you have the hacker's location? It will be something if

Erik trips himself up by hacking from his home or office." I chuckled at the idea.

Lyle responded, "it's in the works. The software is running now. I'll call once I have it." Lyle stood, grabbed his computer, and trotted out of the room.

While the three of us sat in the office hopeful for results, Sanchez, and Schiller stopped in for an update. Unfortunately, their security company business owners checked out, leaving them without a lead. I gave the detectives an overview of Lyle's work and the results we hope to come from it. Sanchez and Schiller agreed to review the case files for evidence and a way to connect Erik to the murders.

I enjoyed lunch with Greta and Jo. It was nice to talk of anything but murders and Madge. No one asked, and I didn't share. As I walked into police headquarters, Jones called. I listened to him while I walked the stairs to our floor. He gave my gut a blow because Erik produced receipts, food, and gas, one hotel receipt, confirming his alibi for the murders. Jones accepted the receipts, and they looked normal, but he has several people working on confirming the validity.

"How did Erik act? Was he nice or mad that we made him produce documents?" I asked Jones.

Jones chuckled and said, "he acted jovial. It was strange. He asked about Jo and if he could meet her again and help us with the hacker. Erik made a point of telling me that Lyle gave him his business card."

"Ugh. Did he call Lyle?"

"Not that I'm aware. Erik kept referring to Conner and Jo. Every time he mentioned Conner, his facial tic occurred."

"Let me know what you find out about the receipts. It will shock me if they're not manufactured. My guess is he's had this planned for a while. Also, see if your guys can find the video supporting Erik's receipt. That would be indisputable proof."

"Good idea, Ryker. I'll do it. Talk later." Jones ended the call, and I repeated our conversation to the group.

Since Jo and Greta took the elevator, I reviewed my conversation with Jones. They want video, too, not just a receipt. I sat at my desk and stared at Jo's worksheet. I went back to the victim's dates of death. They were in no order. The dates were chosen when the killer had a street number in mind. That wouldn't help us nab the killer. Then my eyes shifted from dates of death to the location. I checked off the cities, then my mind raced through ideas. The killer will strike Dallas next.

"Jo, the killer will be in Dallas in November. They're up next for a murder. Then he'll travel to Houston."

With gigantic eyes, Jo stared at me. "How do you know that? The killer has been all over Texas."

After I explained my logic, Jo nodded in agreement. "Now what? We wait around for November."

"We're working on that. Jones might be our best bet on catching the killer. If we can dispute his alibi, we have reason to bring him in for questioning. From there, we can ask a judge for a warrant for his vehicles. I want a fiber from his vehicles so we can compare them. If they match, we can put him at the scene of multiple murders."

"I like it, but I don't expect Erik to go down easy. If he's as smart as you say, he has a backup plan."

My text alert sounded as I nodded. Glancing down, I cringed. Madge's dad texted me about the final test. It's scheduled for 3:00 pm, and we should have our answer by 5:00 pm. When I raised my eyes, Jo knew what the text was about. "Oh, Ryker. Leave this place and go be with Madge."

I heeded her instructions and left without giving Greta a notice. I couldn't because I didn't know what to say. The trip to the hospital was slow. Afternoon rush hour was underway as I made my way to join Madge's parents. My heart told me what was coming, and I braced for it.

Madge's parents sat in their spots. I sat next to Madge's dad. No one spoke because we were expecting earth-shattering news. When you know bad news is coming, there doesn't seem to be much to say.

An hour later, a nurse escorted us to Madge's room. The doctor entered a few minutes later and gave us the dreaded news. Madge would never wake. Her organs are shutting down, and her brain has no movement. The doctor sedated Madge's mom because she couldn't bear to hear the news. I asked the doctor to leave Madge until her mom could say her goodbyes.

While her mom rested in a nearby room, I discussed the situation with Madge's dad. I told him Madge's last wishes. He grinned, saying her mom would be pleased.

We waited a few hours for Madge's mom to settle, then all three of us gathered around Madge's bedside for the last time. A nurse turned the machines off, and Madge was gone within the hour. Her body couldn't hold on any longer.

I listened to her mom weep as she held Madge's hand. Then, when I couldn't hear it anymore, I left. Even when you know it's coming, it's a blow to your heart.

Another trip home but this one, I had my answer. Madge requested no funeral. She asked to be buried next to her parents wherever that might be. She was unsure where I'd end up if she died first. Now, I wonder myself. Can I stay in Ft. Worth?

I paced the house looking at the things Madge purchased to decorate our first house. Since I didn't know when Madge's parents would arrive, I spent time in our bedroom. I touched things we bought on our honeymoon trip, and I looked at pictures on our computer. In my own way, I made peace with her death.

Later, as I laid in bed, I heard the doorknob rattle as Madge's parents entered, probably for the last time. Tomorrow, I'd tell them to take whatever they wanted of their daughter's things. Then, I'd pack the rest and donate it.

After Madge's death, I called no one, not even Jo. My family knew nothing yet, not even of the accident. My mom was one to jump in and try to make everything all right, and this time, I knew she couldn't. So I didn't call. My dad and brothers serve our country. Dad is in Texas, but my brothers are in Germany, or at least that's the last place I knew. Finally, I rolled over and decided to call everyone tomorrow.

The last time I looked at the clock, it glowed at 3:00 am. I woke at 7:00 am. I've operated on less and was grateful for the four hours of sleep, but I felt like I moved in slow motion. Nothing seemed real. I showered, hoping that would help.

Before I went downstairs to face Madge's parents, I made my calls. Jo was first. She wanted to come over until I reminded her of Madge's parents. We agreed to talk later. Then I called Greta. She cried. Something I never expected. She said she'd notify the team for me, then she said to take as much time as I needed. I shocked her when I said I'd be back tomorrow. She questioned me but then refrained. I told her Jo was in charge of the team, but I'd be available for emergencies. She didn't comment, other than saying okay.

My last call was to my mom. That was hard. Mom broke down in sobs, then she got angry because I didn't call sooner. Finally, I gave in to her as she wanted to notify the rest of the family. I wasn't sure how to reach my brothers, anyway.

When I made it downstairs, Madge's parents sat at the bar drinking coffee. After I slowly sipped my coffee, I told them about Madge's things and suggested they look around and take whatever they wanted. They both nodded, and her dad expressed gratitude for my hospitality.

I drank coffee, cup after cup, while I listened to Madge's parents rummage through our things. While there wasn't anything to hide, it still felt weird. Finally, I made a copy of Madge's last wishes and placed them in an envelope for her dad.

They agreed to send me pictures of Madge's grave since there wouldn't be a funeral.

We said our goodbyes at lunchtime amongst tears and hugs. Then, I was lost, so I drove to the gym. While running on the treadmill, I thought of everything I'd need to handle once Madge's death certificate was ready. That thought was daunting. Then the realization hit me I was a widower. No one should be labeled that in their thirties. Again, life dealt me another lousy hand, and I wondered how many more I could take.

Chapter 12

The gym helped me release pent-up frustrations, but I still carried an uneasiness. On my drive home, I contemplated calling Jo but decided against it. I needed the time to myself. As I strolled through the house, I noticed Madge's parents had taken many of Madge's things, which I was grateful, but I smelled her perfume when I walked into the closet. That would pass in time, but how long could I enter this closet and not think of Madge.

Our clothes hung on opposite sides of the closet. So, at least, I knew what needed packing. I took several of Madge's garments from the closet and placed them in a box when I stopped myself. What was I doing, and could I do it? Maybe it was just too soon.

I looked around the room and crawled into bed, pulling the blanket to my chin, and fell into a restless sleep. Dreams invaded my mind as old ones returned with a vengeance. These weren't pleasant dreams. These dreams brought vicious memories. Dreams I had when I served in the military. When the IED exploded, it jolted me awake. I sat in bed with a sweat shine and the covers wrapped around me, staring at my room because it felt too real.

After another shower, my stomach reminded me to eat. I hadn't eaten since the day before. Instead of eating alone, I called Jo. I surprised her by the call, and she agreed to eat with me. I picked her up, and we drove to a restaurant on the outskirts of town because I wasn't in a mood to make pleasantries with people we knew. This restaurant sits next to a lake, and the views are worth the drive.

Dinner was delicious as we chatted over a steak meal. Once the server cleared the dishes, I talked, and Jo let me. I shared Madge's wishes, and Jo nodded and stated, "that's the way to do things." Jo told me she doesn't want a funeral because she doesn't understand them any more than I did. I wonder if Jo has written her last wishes.

When I dropped her off at home, I wanted to stay, but I couldn't stay away from my house forever. I'll have to face it, and it might as well be now. When I entered, the house was eerily quiet. As I closed the door, I stared at the doorknob and grinned. If it rattled in the night now, I'd know I had a problem. Then, I went to each room and glanced inside. Do I stay here? Can I stay here? Then the thought hit me. Maybe I should sell this place and move into something smaller. Who needs a four-bedroom house? We bought this intending to raise kids here. Sadness took over, so to escape it, I went to sleep.

At 3:00 am, my phone rings. Instead of ignoring it and rolling over, I peek at the time and then the number. Cabello's number lit up the screen. I sat up as I answered. Cabello is tense as he tells me Detective Jones didn't check in tonight with dispatch. Jones had Erik under surveillance again, but he was only staying until midnight. Then the gut clencher, Cabello told me Jones never made it home.

With my mind reeling, I have a three-way call with Jo and Greta. We discuss options. Then Greta sends Jo and me to Dallas. It was more for support because we knew very little about Dallas other than a few nightspots and less about Jones. But it wouldn't hurt to scour the area and see if we picked up on anything unusual. We wanted to see Erik's business and home, anyway. This would provide us the opportunity to see it in person.

I called Cabello and told him we were on our way. It shocked him we would come to Dallas, but he sounded grateful too. We would be there by 6:00 am since it's only forty-two miles from Ft. Worth to their headquarters.

In the early hour, traffic was light. Jo talked a little as we drove the city streets. Dallas is a beautiful city in the dark. When we arrived, Cabello met us at the door to let us inside. "Bartley, Samples. Thanks for coming. We still have no word from Jones or his car. We've tried pinging his cell phone, and the last known cell tower was around Erik's business at 11:00 pm. Then it goes silent at 12:05 pm. The last check-in from Jones occurred at 10:00 pm. He told the dispatcher his location, then he chuckled and said the guy must work late."

I pondered the information. "At 10:00 pm, he was okay because he talked to dispatch. When was he supposed to check-in again?"

"Midnight. That's when we called off the surveillance, regardless of Erik's location."

"Are we assuming something happened between 11:00 pm and midnight?" I asked.

"Unfortunately, that's the only assumption we have. We also tried the car GPS, and it's not operational. Last known address was Erik's business." Cabello stated as his eyes told me he expected the worst.

"Cabello, we'd like to drive by Erik's business and house. Can you drive us, or if not, we can find it?"

"Let's go. If I find out this caused Jones any harm, I want to be the one to slap the cuffs on him! I imagined nothing like this would happen. Jones told me from the start that he didn't like Erik because he felt Erik thought he was smarter than the rest. I wish I had listened."

As we exited the front door, Commander Tiller met us. He shared he issued a BOLO for Detective Jones' vehicle. That was a solemn moment for all. We climbed into Cabello's car in silence. He took us to Erik's business first since its closest to headquarters. I shared my desire to gather fibers from Erik's vehicle, and while everyone agreed, no one offered an idea of how to get them.

Erik's business address was in an industrial area but well-kept. These buildings held retail or office space in the front with workspace in the rear. The front wall of each building was brick, while the sides were metal. Each building had a concrete entrance with flowering trees in the front. Signage attached to the front wall simply stated Erik Cleggman Enterprises. I imagine that left people wondering what kind of enterprises he has in that building.

We didn't park our vehicle because we didn't want Erik knowing we were anywhere near his business. Instead, we parked two buildings away and on the opposite side of the street. Cabello handed me a pair of binoculars. I scanned the area, then I passed them to Jo. We discussed surveillance points, and we chose the most likely spot for Jones. I sketched the buildings and the parking lot.

Next, Cabello drove ten minutes to Erik's house. The neighborhood was typical of most. Erik's home was a two-story with a two-car garage. The lots were smaller than mine, forcing the homes closer together. From the road, I could see the house behind Erik's facing another street. I saw no way for Erik to kill Jones at his home without the neighbor's noticing or hearing something.

"Cabello, I need one more trip to Erik's business. Jones' car is there somewhere. It might not be in Erik's building, but it's in the area." I stated as I studied my sketch.

Jo moaned. "I agree, Ryker. Lots more places to stow a car."

Cabello glanced at me as he turned the car for Erik's business. "How can you be so sure?"

"It would be easier to dispose of a vehicle while in town instead of a neighborhood. Besides, there are a ton of warehouses back here. Erik might know of vacant ones, and they would make perfect dumping grounds." I explained.

We pulled into the industrial park and drove around several buildings. The storage or workshop areas offered no street-level windows. Therefore, the only way to determine the warehouse contents will be to enter each one, and without a warrant, we must have permission. With the number of buildings in this park, that will take hours to enter each one. Maybe Tiller could help with extra officers.

"I suggest we return to the office and ask Tiller for extra help. There's no way for you, Morton, and Lopez to handle this alone. Of course, we'll help too."

Cabello drove us back to the office. His mind was on Jones. The muscles in his jaws popped a few times, so neither of us spoke. I texted Jo asking if she had any other ideas, she replied with a frowny face.

A shock waited for us as Tiller called us to join him in his office. There were two men in dark suits and white shirts standing to the side of his desk. I knew exactly who they were. Jo pinched me on the back of the arm as we followed Tiller into the office.

Tiller introduced the two Feds to us, and we shook hands. They asked for an update on Detective Jones, and they questioned if Jones worked the serial killer case. During that split second, many things ran through my mind. My first thought was someone in the Dallas office leaked information to the FBI. That made me mad.

I grabbed my phone from my pocket and acted like Greta called. "Tiller, this is Huxley. Jo can explain where we are with the case." I winked at Jo as I turned my back to the room and left. Jo's face was hilarious, and I imagine she'll tell me how funny it was later.

My finger throbbed because I pushed Greta's speed dial button too hard. Anger flowed through my body like it hasn't in years. Greta answered, and I unleashed. She was just as mad as me but too far away to make a difference. Greta emphasized holding some of our evidence close and ensuring they understand we're not giving the FBI our serial killer case because it doesn't warrant federal involvement yet.

I returned to the office within minutes and explained Commander Huxley called to check-in with us.

Commander Tiller had a strange facial expression. I couldn't decide if he was mad or worried. Then a thought hit me. Is Tiller the leak? If so, he's using this case to fast forward his career. I faced the group then asked, "are we finished here?"

An FBI agent asked me if I spotted the serial killer's pattern. I shrugged, and Jo spouted yes, probably retaliating against me for leaving her. Then the agent asked for details. I explained the dates of death and how they correlate with the weekday and street addresses. Without trying, I impressed the Feds. They asked to be updated on the case, and then the lead agent asked me for a business card. Luckily, I had one, but I had to dig for it. When they exited the office, Jo stared at me because she didn't understand the meeting either.

Cabello, Jo, and I walked to his desk as I tried to find the premise for the meeting. Why would the Feds stop in and ask for an update without asking for the file? I've never known that to happen, and they've taken several cases from Ft. Worth. We relinquished a rape case and a kidnapping, but both involved multiple states. That I can explain, but this visit is without meaning.

"My suggestion is to print an aerial view of Erik's business location then a wider angle showing the number of warehouses in the area. Once we have that, we'll approach Tiller with our idea. What do you think?" I asked Cabello and Jo.

Both agreed, so we moved ahead and tried to put the unwanted visit out of our heads. We made several prints to accommodate the number of warehouses. There were more than I expected. Cabello asked us to join him. I cringed because I wanted to call Greta and discuss our situation. But we followed Cabello into Tiller's office, then Morton and Lopez joined.

Tiller questioned Morton and Lopez, "did you guys find anything useful?"

"Not one thing. Jones is gone. It's like he vanished. We found a camera on the corner of one warehouse that we'd like to see the video. Our issue is the warehouse appears vacant, so I'm unsure if the camera is operational or not." Morton explained as Tiller nodded.

Then, Tiller looked at Cabello and said, "what's on your mind, Cabello?"

Cabello explained our thought process to the group. He provided a concise delivery, and everyone understood why the warehouses are critical. Finally, Morton asked, "why are we assuming Erik disposed of Jones in a warehouse?" Cabello glanced at me, and I answered.

"Cabello drove us by Erik's house. He lives in a two-story on a small lot in a neighborhood. Someone would have seen Erik or heard the commotion just because of the proximity of the homes. If Erik kills Jones, he still has to remedy the car situation. What better place to hide a body and car than in a warehouse amongst dozens of identical ones?" I glanced at each person in the room. Jo grinned while the others processed the information.

Tiller cleared his throat and agreed. "You're right, Bartley. That would be the perfect place. Our issue is gaining access to each warehouse quickly. I'll see if we have enough evidence for a judge to sign a warrant. I'm not holding my breath on that one. Our Plan B will have officers working in pairs stopping at each warehouse for entry. If the warehouse is vacant, we'll contact the owners and request permission."

All heads nodded, and I felt a sense of relief. "Let us know when you get the word on the warrant. We'll start pulling the tax records for the owner's information to have on standby." I offered as we walked from Tiller's office.

Jo leaned into me, "when can we call Greta?"

I winked then looked at the rest of the team. "Guys, Jo and I need to check-in with Commander Huxley. We'll be right back. Can you point toward coffee?" Everyone pointed down the hall, and we followed their instructions.

Jo said, "my eyes want to close. This has been a long day, and it isn't over yet." Finally, we rounded the corner to a massive break room. The office provided coffee, bottled water, and a few snacks with ample space to enjoy your treats alone.

Once we had our coffee, we moved to the far corner where we could speak freely. Greta answered my call on the first ring. She was eager to hear the news. With the phone on speaker, Jo and I offered commentary about the earlier meeting with the Feds, then our request of Commander Tiller. Greta had no other ideas to offer, so we moved on. Then Greta added, "Sanchez and Schiller reviewed the cases for additional evidence. We have two items. Ortega found a cellphone belonging to a July 2019 victim. Supposedly she used her phone calendar for appointments, but he never followed up on the phone. Has he mentioned anything to either of you about the calendar?"

Jo and I answered, "no." We jotted a note.

Then, Greta continued, "The November 2013 case shows a bloody fingerprint on the kitchen counter. We wanted to compare it with Erik's prints, but Sanchez checked, and we have no prints for Erik in the system since he wasn't in the military nor has he been arrested."

"I like the fingerprint angle. Jo and I will work to get his prints. We're close enough to him we might

stop in and say hello. I'd like his reaction, anyway."
I suggested while glancing at Jo.

Jo added, "maybe Lyle could give us a reason to
visit Erik. Then we need him to give us bottled
water. As long as we don't touch the same area he
did, we'd have his prints."

A smile spread across my face. "You're a genius," I
commented to Jo.

Greta paused before agreeing to the idea. "Call Lyle
and see he can offer a reason to visit Erik. But the
reason must be legitimate. If Erik is smart as you
say, he'll figure out we're on to him, and we don't
want that."

Our call ended with a mood booster. Not only did
we have a plan to get Erik's prints, but we also
gained more evidence. I called Ortega on the cell
phone calendar while Jo spoke with Lyle. Ortega
promised to follow up with the lab today. He and
Brown were meeting with a team member of a local
security company.

Jo's call with Lyle ended with her eyebrows
bunched. "Jo, what is it? Something's wrong."

"Lyle didn't come into work. No one has heard
from him today. Another lab tech is driving to
Lyle's house to see if he's okay." Jo looked at me
with something I don't usually see in her eyes.
She's scared.

"Does Greta know this? We better call her back." I hit redial on my phone, and Greta answered.

"That was fast. What did you find out?" Greta asked.

I shared with her about Lyle's disappearance. The line went silent. She finally spoke with a crackle to her voice.

"Ryker, Jo, we can't let anything happen to Lyle. He's just a kid. I know Jones remains a mystery too, but Lyle is ours. I need your help. Can you come home?"

Jo and I nodded, then Jo spoke. "We'll let Tiller and the guys know what's happening, then we'll come back. They should have enough people to check the warehouses. We'll text when we leave here."

"Greta, I have one thing to check out before we come home. I want to see if Erik is at work today or if he's out of town. If it's the latter, we have a serious problem because I suspect Lyle made Erik nervous, and Erik finished it."

Both ladies offered no comment, so I ended the call. Jo and I walked into Tiller's office and told him the latest. They would handle their missing detective while we worked to find our missing lab tech.

We explained our departure with Cabello, and he wished us well in locating Lyle, and we the same for Jones. Both agreed to leave the communication lines open. Then, Jo and I headed to the car.

When we climbed inside, my first inclination was to drive to Erik's business. I wanted him to see us. But I had no reason for being there other than to make a statement. Jo and I debated whether to call him or visit his business. We called. Jo volunteered, since a lady is less threatening than a man, but they don't know Jo.

Jo dialed Erik's business number, and a young girl answered. When Jo asked to speak with Erik, the girl stated she would transfer the call to his cellphone since he was out of the office. I listened as Jo said they had set a tentative appointment and needed to see if he was still available. The girl told Jo that Erik was in Ft. Worth on business, and she was unsure when he was returning. As soon as Jo ended the call, she looked at me, "let's drive over to Erik's house and see if his work truck is there."

So, we did just that. We walked outside to storm clouds building. There was a noticeable temperature drop as I watched Jo shiver. Neither spoke as we drove to Erik's using a maps app. These directions differed from the others. I've never been able to explain why or how an app knew how to change directions, but I'm glad they can.

There were no trucks in the driveway, and no lights on in the house on arrival. However, his next door neighbor was leaning into her mailbox, and I pulled to the curb. I let my window down, and I asked, "Hi, We're Ft. Worth Detectives Bartley and Samples, and we're looking for Erik. Do you know where he might be?"

"No. He always lets me know when he'll be away, but I heard him leave in his truck in the middle of the night. I have an infant, and it was feeding time. I peeked out the window in time to see him back his work truck from the drive then pull away, and I haven't seen him since."

"Thanks for your help." Once the window closed, I looked at Jo.

Jo shook her head. "He's in Ft. Worth." Her voice sounds scared. She feared for Lyle, and I did too. It's time to return to Ft. Worth, and I considered bringing Conner into the office again and share our suspicions about his friend. But then again, I don't trust him either. Somehow, my answer lies with Erik's fingerprints.

We rode in silence as ideas bounced around our heads until my phone rang. I pushed the button on my steering wheel to answer the phone. We listened as Ortega told us his murder victim had an appointment scheduled in her phone calendar with EC before her murder. Their lab tech confirmed her phone showed only one appointment with EC and no phone contact card matching EC.

I didn't get into the details of Jones and Lyle with Ortega. We would schedule a meeting with everyone for that discussion, but I wanted more information on Lyle.

Jo's text message sounded. She fished her phone from her bag and read it. "Greta sent us Lyle's address, and she suggests we visit his home first before we go to the office."

"I'm worried about Lyle. Would Erik kill Lyle? Lyle only met Erik once." Jo asked

"If Erik is our killer, he'll kill anyone that gets in his way. Lyle would be tops on his list if Erik saw how close Lyle was to finding Erik's hack job. Lyle kept Erik's original computer code, and if Erik knows that there's a chance Lyle is already dead."

Jo didn't comment, but she surveyed the surroundings as we pulled into Lyle's condo complex. We found his condo tucked into the middle row of identical condos. This is a massive complex. If I sold my house, I know I couldn't live in a complex like this.

Lyle's car sat in his assigned space. We walked around the car and found nothing. The hood was cold, so we suspected he parked it a while ago. With the front door locked, we followed a path on the building's side that led us to the rear of the condo.

The condo boasted a small, paved patio with a table, chairs and a grill. I tried the door, and it didn't budge. I ran my hand over the door frame and came away with nothing. Jo lifted potted plants, searching for a key. When she found nothing, she moved to the rocks. Three rocks from the door, she got lucky.

We entered Lyle's condo expecting an alarm to sound. When nothing happened, we moved forward. Jo walked to the eating area while I inspected the family room. "Ryker, there are dishes in the sink, but otherwise, everything looks normal."

"Until you come in here. Pillows and papers lay scattered on the floor next to a laptop computer charging cord. But I see no laptop." I said as I turned circles taking in the room. Nothing else seemed disturbed.

We took the steps to the second floor. Lyle's bedroom appeared lived in, but nothing suspicious. The other bedroom sat untouched. "Jo, Erik took Lyle from downstairs with his laptop. Lyle is alive because Erik needs him."

Jo's eyes brightened. "So, if Erik took him, where is he? If Erik isn't at work and his home was dark, does Erik own another property?"

"Interesting question. Let's look at that when we get back to the office."

When we left Lyle's, we locked the doors as we went through the front door. A guy stood by our vehicle waiting for us. He said, "who are you, and where is Lyle?"

I stepped forward and stated, "Ft. Worth Detectives Bartley and Samples. And you are?"

The guy's face fell, "I'm sorry. I heard two guys yelling. When I looked out the window, Lyle stepped into a van. I ran downstairs, and by the time I opened my front door, the van pulled away."

Jo's head whipped around and faced me. "Can you describe the driver?"

"All I saw was brown hair, and he was Caucasian. His face was turned away from me. The van was a work truck, but I didn't see a logo. What's going on?" The guy pleaded.

"It's an ongoing investigation," I stated and thanked the guy for the information. Somehow, I felt relieved knowing Lyle left alive, and while I know that doesn't prove he's still alive, I liked these odds.

We drove away and headed for the office. Greta met us at our desks and ushered us into the conference room. Sanchez and Schiller waited for us. I described the scene at Lyle's, including the neighbor's statement. We had his name and number in case we needed more information.

Greta and Schiller agreed with me about Lyle's survival chances. But then, Greta threw us a curveball. "I have someone willing to help us, but I wanted your thoughts before I agreed."

Jo glanced at Ryker then back to Greta as she continued, "Tiller shared with his FBI friends about Lyle's disappearance. One agent you met in Dallas is supposedly a cyber sleuth. He's willing to take Lyle's place in tracking Erik's hacking abilities. If Lyle has a security system, I feel sure Erik hacked into his system and disabled it."

I asked the following question because the three detectives sitting beside me had the same one. "Is the FBI taking over the investigation?"

"They tell me they are not taking the case from us, but they offered their services. These FBI agents are local, so they want to help." Greta explained, and she waited for an answer.

While I pondered the scenario, the others shrugged their shoulders. Could the FBI give us additional help that we didn't have before? Their systems are more sophisticated than ours.

"I'll agree if he understands his boundaries." Greta nodded in acknowledgment.

Then she said, "I'll make the call." She left us staring at each other.

"Jo, check with the property records and see if Erik owns more property," I stated. Then I turned my attention to Sanchez and Schiller. "Good work on the evidence. Ortega called, and his murder victim had a scheduled appointment on her cell phone with someone carrying the initials EC. Unfortunately, her contacts provided no name for EC, and we're still trying to find Erik's prints."

Schiller asked about Jones. I gave them the rundown on the investigation and the warehouses. Then Greta popped into the room. "FBI Agent Westerly is on his way upstairs. He asked for access to a computer because he wanted to check CCTV footage for the white van. If they can track it, we might have Lyle's location."

My eyebrows shot upward, as did Jo's. Sanchez and Schiller's mouths made an O as Greta made her statement. Greta chuckled when she saw our faces.

Five minutes later, Agent Westerly joined us in the conference room. He was older than me but not by much, and he carried an air of military service. When he looked at me, he nodded like he knew me.

"That was quick, Westerly. Were you sitting in the parking lot?" I glanced at him as I gathered his laptop.

Sheepishly, he met my eyes. "No, I was in the lobby." Everyone snickered at his reply. I already liked him.

I handed him a laptop and left him in the conference room after explaining we'd be around the office if he needed anything. Jo worked at her computer searching for more property owned by Erik Cleggman. Before I made it to my desk, Jo sighed as her search was a bust. "Ryker, I checked Erik's name, personal, and business, and he owns his home and the business location, but nothing else."

"Not surprising, but we needed to check," I stated, but a question popped into my mind. "Would Erik keep Lyle at his house? I know the place was dark, and the neighbor admitted to not seeing him since he left in the night, but could he?"

Jo considered my questions before replying, "anything with this guy is possible. But if Lyle is still alive, he would have to keep him somewhere so he could access his computer."

I jumped up, leaving Jo at her desk with shock on her face. I trotted to the conference room to speak with Westerly. "Agent Westerly, is it possible to trace Lyle's IP address for his location?"

"Absolutely, if the computer has internet service, we can find it. I'll need Lyle's IP address." Westerly glanced at me.

Since I was unsure how to get Lyle's IP address, I walked into Greta's office, and she spoke with the crime lab. I raised my hand and asked her to place them on hold for a second. Then, I explained my request. Returning to the call, Greta relayed the request for Lyle's IP address.

Greta's contact produced the address in seconds, and I headed back to Westerly. After I passed him the sticky note, he said to give him a little time. I watched him enter the IP address into a long search bar.

When Westerly hit the enter button, he asked me to sit, so I did. We talked while he searched CCTV footage for the white van. Then, Westerly asked me about my unique gift of seeing patterns. I don't like sharing about my brainpower for some reason, but I felt compelled to tell him my story.

As I spoke, he listened intently, as if he understood my past. When I finished, he leaned down and raised his left pants leg, revealing a prosthetic. Our eyes met as kindred spirits.

Westerly told me his story, and we shared much the same experiences and misery in our military careers, but I came away with a gift, and he didn't. He was jealous.

Injuries cut our military careers short, and we had to pick a different line of work. We both gravitated to police work. Westerly asked, "Bartley, did you ever consider working with the FBI?"

"Nope. It wasn't even on my radar. So why would I have considered them? I've had no formal training in anything but guns." We chuckled over that one.

Over the next few hours, I learned CCTV techniques, and the more I learned about technology, the more I liked it. It gave us another avenue that we could do ourselves. I'm all about handling things myself instead of depending on others.

Jo stepped into the room and watched us from the doorway. "hey guys, anyone for coffee?"

We said yes at the same time. "Westerly, how do you take yours? I've made enough for Ryker that I don't need to ask him." This brought a chuckle.

"Black works. Thanks." Westerly's gaze returned to the computer. "Found the van. It's five blocks from Lyle's condo heading to the interstate."

"Erik took Lyle to Dallas," I whispered more to myself than anyone.

Chapter 13

Jo returned with the coffee. We took our cups and took a sip. Then I told Jo about the van and my assumption on Lyle being in Dallas.

"Makes sense to me since he lives and works there," Jo said as she left with her phone to her ear.

While Westerly worked on the computer, Jo and I shared our need for Erik's prints and truck fibers. Our lack of evidence is troublesome because we have no physical evidence placing Erik at any of our murder scenes. Jo mentioned the bloody fingerprint, but we need Erik's for comparison.

Westerly glanced up from his computer, "we'll find a way to get this guy." Then he turned quiet as he checked on the search for Lyle's IP address location. As we waited for the results, he glanced at me and offered his condolences for Madge's death. It shocked me he knew, but it shouldn't have because he obviously knew more about me than I did about him.

We listened as Jo ended her call. She stuck her head in the room and said, "Tiller didn't get the search warrant for the warehouses. They're preparing to search each one."

With a furrowed brow, Westerly asked for an explanation. Jo explained our warehouse theory as Westerly nodded his acknowledgment. "So, you both think Erik is hiding Jones in a warehouse?"

"Yes, I do. It's the most logical. We have an aerial view of the area if you want to see it."

"Show me." Westerly groaned. Then he stated, "The van disappeared. I'll backtrack and see where he turned off."

Jo handed me the aerial maps, and we laid them out in order. Westerly stood over the maps eyeing the layout. "I'm assuming the red star signifies Erik's warehouse." We nod. "Let me make a call." He states.

He stepped away to make the call while we stared at each other. Greta texted me, so I slipped away, leaving Jo in the room. When I returned, Jo and Westerly sat huddled together. I moaned. Jo is my partner, and it shouldn't bother me when I see her close to another man, but it does.

Jo blurted out, "Westerly got the warrant for the warehouses, and he just emailed it to Tiller." Jo grinned for the first time in a while. I noticed her lipstick was fresh too. Uh oh. I feel a competition coming. What will Westerly say when he hears about my feelings for Jo? My eyes bounce between Jo and Westerly, and when I see Westerly's expression, I decide he'll understand, but he's falling for those eyes too.

"Does Tiller know about the warrant?" I asked.

With a nod, Jo says, "I called him and told him to expect it. It thrilled him to have it saying how much time it would save. They have no new clues on Jones."

"I'm guessing he's dead because Erik got nervous when he spotted Jones watching him. Jones offered nothing of use for Erik either, unlike Lyle. Erik thinks Lyle will help steer the police away from him."

Westerly nodded as he clicked a few keys on the laptop. He's working to locate the white van again. "Here he is. But I wonder where he went. Who can pull up a street map for me of his last known location and now?"

"I can." As I got to work, I realized what he was trying to do. He wants to know where the van stopped after it exited the interstate. Once I had the information on my laptop, we sat side by side so he could view both screens. "It would be nice if Erik stopped for gas at a station with cameras."

With a chuckle, Westerly offered, "you figured me out, Bartley. You're better at this than you think."

While Westerly worked his magic on the CCTV footage, I texted Cabello to update their warehouse search. Within moments, I had a reply that the investigation was underway. They had enough teams to start on both ends of the industrial park, hoping to finish today if the occupants cooperated.

I shared with Westerly and Jo, giving thanks to Westerly for his help. He grinned and offered, "it's what I do. But I can't find the van. If he stopped for anything, it must have been a small convenience store."

Jo jumped on it, "I'll work on that end and see if I can find where they stopped. Give me what information you have." She reached her hand to me, and our fingers touched. Something that hasn't happened in weeks. I watched her eyes do that thing, and I grinned. She took the papers from me, smiled, and exited the room.

When I turned back, Westerly stared at me. "Anything you need to share, Bartley?"

I shrugged my shoulders and said, "not really." But I know he had questions about my relationship with Jo. If he could spot it so easily, so could everyone else, which could pose a problem if we moved ahead with our feelings.

With Madge's death so fresh, I was unsure when I'd be ready, but I didn't want to see her give up on me, either. I still had things to work through, but I'd be ready when I was comfortable with it. Now to tell her, so she didn't leave me for Westerly.

While I wanted alone time with Jo, Westerly suggested lunch, so we took Westerly to our favorite lunchtime restaurant. Jo gave me a smile while I entered the lot, and I replied with a wink. We enjoyed great food and conversation. Westerly joined our group, and it feels like he's been here forever. We learned Westerly works out of the Dallas FBI field office, and he's not married. I studied Jo's face when he admitted to it, but I couldn't read it. She also knew I watched her.

As we finished, Cabello sent a text explaining they checked four warehouses and nothing. No signs of Jones or his vehicle. He'd reach out later once they inspected the others.

Now, I questioned my idea. Was I too rash in my assumption? But then, I backtracked my thought process and decided I wasn't. Jones is in a warehouse. We just have to find him.

Back at the office, Westerly studied Lyle's IP address as it bounced around the globe. Westerly called a computer analyst friend for direction. While he spoke on the phone, I stood behind his back, studying the map. I leaned over and pointed to a spot on the computer screen. Westerly stops his conversation and glances at me.

"Bartley, what do you see?"

"He's here. More lines are intersecting here than anywhere else on the map."

I clearly impressed Westerly. He described the scenario with the analyst, then two minutes later, the analyst confirmed my choice. The analyst gave us a few tips to narrow down the area since it provided most of Dallas. However, I noticed both Erik's home and business are in the same area.

Struggling with the idea of Erik keeping Lyle at his house still bothered me. So, I stepped out and shared my thoughts with Westerly. He gave it some thought, looked at the map again, and agreed with me. It is a plausible scenario, but we had no reason to search Erik's house yet.

"Westerly, could Lyle send a coded message through his computer while working for Erik?"

I watched as Westerly's head tilted side to side, "I can't answer that, but I'll call my guy back. He's been an analyst for years. If it's possible, he'll know it." He picked up his phone, dialed, and left a message.
Jo called for me, so I left Westerly with the CCTV footage again and his work on narrowing down the location of Lyle's IP address. That's most promising for me.

When I sat at my desk facing Jo, she had a strange expression. "What's wrong? Did something happen?"

"Something happened, but it's not case related. I wanted you to be the first to know." She stopped and caught her breath.

Waiting patiently is hard for me. But I'm glad I'm did. When she told me she had a date with Conner, I swallowed hard. I was mad. Mad at Conner for asking and mad at Jo for accepting. "Well, that was unexpected." I rubbed my hand through my hair then around my neck.

She leaned over and gave me a half-hearted excuse about the case, but I think she liked the guy too. There was no denying the two had eyes for each other when he came to the office for our interview. But that didn't mean I had to like it.

Jo left the office early, leaving me with Westerly. He asked me what was going on, and I told him. Westerly had a simple time reading people, and he knew this was troublesome for me. "Let's follow Jo."

I stared at him with my eyebrows raised. Then he continued, "at least, we'd be close enough if something happened."

My insides quivered because she would never forgive me for tailing her. Westerly witnessed my internal struggle, "Blame it on me, Bartley."

When I looked at him, I grinned and replied, "I will."

Since Jo already left the office, we did too since she didn't share what time she expected Conner. We wanted to be in place when he showed. And we were. Conner picked Jo up at her place shortly after we parked. When she stepped through the door, I noticed she wore new jeans, a different t-shirt, and a jacket, and with the weather turning cooler, she traded flat shoes for boots.

Jo never looked our way, so I couldn't decide if she knew we were there. We followed them to a restaurant on the outskirts of town. Once the pair settled, we drove thru the nearest fast-food place we found. While Jo ate in style, we ate in the car, discussing the case.

Westerly pointed out the most promising leads are Lyle's IP address and the Dallas warehouse searches. I agreed, but I still wanted to inspect Erik's warehouse. While I didn't see him hiding Jones there, I hoped to find physical evidence, like fibers.

We perked up when Conner and Jo exited the restaurant ninety minutes later. He drove her home and never left his vehicle as Jo walked to her front door. "What kind of man doesn't walk a lady to her door?" Westerly quipped.

I didn't offer a response. Instead, I grinned because I didn't want her to like him, anyway.

We headed back to the office, and I dropped Westerly at his car to drive to Dallas. I drove home with ideas swirling in my head, some about Jo and some about the case. As I entered my house, the silence bothered me less every day. I never realized how tired I was until I laid down. Sleep came quickly and without dreams for once.

My alarm sounded, and I shot up from the bed because it startled me. From the looks of the bed, I never turned over during the night, and that's unusual for me. My head returned to the pillow as I pondered another day. Glancing to the window, I saw rain clouds, and I hoped that wasn't a precursor to my day.

I made it to the office first, followed by Westerly, then Jo. When we settled into the conference room, I asked, "How was your date, Jo?" Westerly stared at me as if I'd lost my mind.

She grinned as she made eye contact, "you two should know since you were there." Then she stomped out of the room, leaving us staring at each other.

"That went well, Bartley. Wonder when she spotted us?" Westerly said as he shook his head.

"Knowing her, she saw us as she walked to Conner's car." Closing my eyes, I shook my head. I know a tongue lashing is forthcoming. I dreaded it.

Westerly had an overnight thought about Lyle's IP. He wanted to see if Lyle connected to the system at the same time during the day. If so, we would connect too and send a message to him instead of waiting for Lyle to send us a message. Since it might be too dangerous for Lyle to instigate the message.

While Westerly worked with his idea, I chatted with Cabello. So far, the searches have found nothing useful for our case. A few people have security cameras, but they store their files off-site. They've requested the files, but we've yet to receive them.

"Cabello don't hold your breath for those files. If Erik can hack into a security company system, he can do the same for the security cameras. But we still need a look at them. We might get lucky. He can't be right all the time."

I looked at Jo's worksheet again. Every day we moved a little closer to November. If we don't catch him now, we might not have another shot until July of next year, and I, for one, don't want to wait that long.

The team had lunch together. Sanchez and Schiller got along well with Westerly too, and I was glad to use them to buffer Jo and myself. While she was still mad at me for tailing her, her features softened as the day progressed.

On our way into the office, my cell phone rang. I plucked it from my pocket and answered. My breath caught in my throat as I wanted to scream. But, instead, I held it together long enough to tell the team Cabello found Jones in a Dallas warehouse. Jo's eyes filled with tears as she worked to keep them from spilling over, and the guys turned their eyes down.

"I'll share with Greta, and I'm going to Dallas in fifteen minutes if anyone wants to tag along." I stepped off the elevator and walked into Greta's office. She knew Jones was dead when she saw my face.

Fifteen minutes later, I walked to my car to find the team standing around it. I climbed into the driver's seat with Westerly in the passenger seat. Jo sat in the middle of the back seat between Schiller and Sanchez. She planned it so we could look at each other on the trip.

Our road trip to the warehouses took us forty-two minutes. I concentrated on driving with intermittent glances at Jo. She did the same, and a few times, our eyes met. Her eyes held a sadness I hadn't seen before. I wanted to reach my hand back and touch her just to let her know everything would be okay. Instead, I pulled into the parking lot packed with police cars, figuring this was our crime scene.

We stepped out of the car into a fine drizzle. With none of us prepared for rain, we searched for cover.

A few of the officers I recognized from past meetings, but I couldn't find Cabello. I craned my neck over the crowd when I caught Cabello's hand waving in the air. He stood next to the roll-up door. When we were in earshot, I expressed sorrow for Jones and the department. Then I asked Cabello to give us a rundown of the scene before we saw it.

Just as we started, the medical examiner arrived. I asked Cabello to hold them off to give us a chance to look at the scene before they removed Jones because seeing a body firsthand is better than studying photos. He obliged.

We walked to Jones' car first. On the way, I noticed unmarked boxes stacked along one wall covered in dust. I wondered if this warehouse is still in use because it seemed someone scattered things around without reason. The team surveyed the area too.

Sanchez followed my train of thought when he asked, "is this warehouse vacant? Dust covers everything in here, and it's messing with my sinuses."

I nodded but kept walking as Sanchez started sneezing. In the middle of the warehouse sat Jones, still inside the car but in the passenger seat. Jo beat me to this observation, "Ryker, Jones is in the passenger seat. If the killer drove the car here, we might have a chance for fibers." This improved her mood by giving her hope.

Cabello joined us as Jo made her statement. Then he answered, "The crime scene unit found fibers in the seat and floorboard in their initial inspection. My guess is they match the other fibers. They also found a portion of a torn receipt that apparently stuck to the killer's shoe. It's not much, but it might be useful too."

"I'd like to think Jones didn't die in vain. He might be the one to solve this thing." Westerly added, and I concurred because I liked Jones. But I considered what would have happened if I hadn't mentioned Erik so soon, if I had waited until I had more evidence tying him to the murders, would Jones still be alive?

As I studied Jones, the killer shot him point-blank in the left side of his head with powder burns circling the wound. I surmise the killer spotted Jones during his surveillance, slipped out of the office, came up from behind the car while Jones sat in it, placed his gun against Jones' head, and fired. With the window down, the killer should have had blood blowback on his clothes and weapon.

My attention turned back to the wound. The bullet hole appears to be a 9 mm caliber, but the medical examiner will confirm. A thought followed my wound inspection. Does Erik own a handgun? I asked the group, and no one knew. So I added that to my list.

Once I asked about Erik owning a gun, Cabello asked the crime lab tech to run a ballistic comparison between Jones' bullet and our murders. If they match, the same killer murdered Jones. No one commented because we all felt this was a given since Jones was surveilling Erik.

Next, the tow truck pulled up to the scene. I couldn't prolong the inevitable, so we relinquished Jones' body to the medical examiner and the car to the crime lab. The faster they left, the faster the results came.

I studied the warehouse some more. By the items stored, I couldn't decide what business occupied it last. There were offices along the far wall, and I meandered to that end. The offices still held desks and filing cabinets, but they were empty. A nice leather chair remained in the middle, and it didn't appear as dusty as the rest of the warehouse. Even the desktop had been cleaned recently.

"Cabello, can you have the crime lab dust for prints in here? It might be a waste, but I'd like to know. The chair and the desk appear cleaner than the rest of the place."

"You're right, Bartley. I'll do that now." He walked off to the other end of the building while the rest of us continued our stroll.

Schiller spoke, "does anyone know how the killer gained access to this place?"

We shook our heads and lifted our shoulders because no one knew the answer. "We'll inspect the door on the way out. There may be a lock or something with telltale signs of tampering."

Once our interior inspection concluded, we walked back out of the same roll-up door. Cabello showed us the lock, and it's intact. "The killer had a key, knows where the owner keeps it or picked the lock without leaving marks. The warehouse was locked when we made entry."

"Do you know who owns this warehouse?" Jo asked Cabello.

"Not without referring to my list, and it's the car. I'll get the information for you." He offered.

Standing in the doorway, I looked both ways. The left took me out of the industrial park and back to town, while the right sent me straight into Erik's warehouse. Everything centers on him. But how can we arrest him without evidence?

When I turned to face the team, I saw Jo shiver, and that's when I realized how chilly the warehouse was without heat. "Ready? There's nothing more to see here." I asked.

We asked Cabello to check-in with us later as Tiller joined the group. Tiller thanked me for finding Jones, and I merely nodded. I didn't find him, but I pointed his team in the area.

Greta called as I settled behind the wheel. I placed my phone on speaker, and we rehearsed the scene for her. She had no questions. It felt good to be some place dry and warmer than the warehouse. I pulled away from the lot when Westerly asked, "Can we drive by Erik's house?"

Jo asked from the back seat, "do you have an idea?"

Westerly turned his head to the left, "I'm working on one. Before we left, I submitted a query on Lyle's IP address. If he logs into the system at the same time every day, I'll send him a message, hoping he sees it and responds." He grinned as he thought about his plan.

Schiller asked, "do you where Lyle is being kept?"

I grinned on that one. "If we did, we would have gotten him out." Everyone chuckled. We needed the laugh.

"Let me rephrase that question. I know you have an idea of Lyle's location. Can you share?"

With a smile, Westerly gave Schiller a quick glance as he sat behind me. "I ran a program on Lyle's IP address. It crisscrossed across the globe, but Bartley found a common spot, so we're centering on that area. That encompasses most of Dallas. We thought if we could get a message to Lyle, then we would have his location."

Sanchez muttered. "I hope Erik doesn't see the message. He might take offense to it."

I glanced at Westerly, who fell silent. "We didn't consider that, Westerly. Would Erik be able to see the message? He's a computer guru too."

"I'm only sending it to Lyle's IP address, so as long as Erik isn't using Lyle's computer, we'll be fine." I thought through Westerly's explanation, and I know every computer carries its own IP address, so there's hope.

We drove by Erik's house, and it looked the same as it did last time I was here. He closed the blinds leaving the house an unoccupied look. There were no papers on the driveway, so either he doesn't subscribe to the newspaper, or he stayed here last night and picked it up on his way out this morning.

Westerly commented, "it would be nice to walk around the house. I'd like to peek into a window or two, even though I bet Lyle is being kept in an upstairs guest bedroom."

"Without a legitimate reason for entering the home, we're stuck. There is no reason to risk it without knowing the end result. I don't want Erik walking away from this because of our inability to be patient." I explained.

Everyone agreed as we made a right turn out of his neighborhood. I looked into the rearview mirror as a white van turned right into the neighborhood. I let out a sigh because I don't want to spook Erik, and it would if he caught us cruising his neighborhood.

We returned to Ft. Worth without incident. Westerly returned to his computer while Jo and I headed for the coffee bar. I asked Sanchez and Schiller to investigate the warehouse owner as we looked into Erik's background for gun ownership.

Late in the afternoon, we reconvened in the conference room. Westerly grinned, so he shared first. "Lyle logs into his computer two times a day. The first time is between eleven and twelve, then four to five, and nothing overnight. So tomorrow, at eleven, I'll be ready."

Westerly's information gave us the boost we needed. If we found Lyle at Erik's house, we could arrest Erik for kidnapping. At least he'd be off the streets.

Then Schiller and Sanchez busted our bubble by sharing Erik had no weapons registered to him, so that idea went nowhere, as did the warehouse owner. The owner is an out-of-state company that had a satellite location in Dallas. The building hasn't been used in years.

Chapter 14

The day ended with our only hope being Westerly. He returned to Dallas, and the rest of the team set out for home. When we exited the door, all eyes turned upward. We spent all day in the drizzle, and it was nice we didn't have to run to our cars since the rain ceased while we were indoors.

My phone rang as I turned right from the lot, and my insides tightened. Since my phone rest in my pocket, I pressed the phone button on my steering wheel. Jo called, and it surprised me when she asked me to dinner. I accepted without a second thought. We could talk interrupted as long as our phones stayed silent.

We met at a local bar not too far from her house. This is one of our favorites whenever we meet. The noise hit me when we entered. Sports played on every TV lining the walls of the joint. Instead of sitting at the bar, like we sometimes do, we chose a corner booth.

Once our server took our orders, Jo looked at me, and my heart rate spiked. She was back, but I didn't let on that I could read her eyes. That was one thing I never wanted to change.

When Jo mentioned the case, I held up my hand to stop her. "No case talks tonight. We've had no time alone time in a while. We need this."

I tried to find the words that I had worked out in my head, but they didn't come. This turned out to be more challenging than I imagined. Finally, after several attempts, I blurted out my feelings to Jo.

It surprised Jo when I told her how I felt. She paused before answering, "I'll wait, Ryker, I'll wait."

I reached across the table, took her hand, and kissed her palm. "Hold on to that for me, Jo."

Tears filled her eyes, and before they tumbled over the edge, our server returned. We ate and laughed through supper. Something about our relationship just feels right, but could it destroy our careers?

Our night ended as Jo pulled out of the lot first. I followed her because I wanted to make sure she made it home safely. Two cars behind me, a white van stayed in the left lane, following us. It seemed odd, so I radioed Jo through dispatch to have a record of the van.

When Jo returned the radio call, she instructed me to go around the block while she entered her garage. She wanted to see if the white van parked nearby. While I didn't want to lose sight of her, I followed her lead. Halfway around the block, Jo radioed she was inside and couldn't spot the car. My eyes shifted to the rearview mirror, and the white van followed me instead of Jo.

I called dispatch and advised them the white van continued to follow me. They rolled back up in case I needed it. I listened as patrol officers took the call then they activated their lights and sirens. A few seconds later, I heard Sanchez report to dispatch that he would assist in my call.

The van stayed two cars behind me on the trip home. I tried to see the driver, but the darkness prevented me. I turned into a gas station outside my neighborhood because I didn't want to take a gunfight into a crowded subdivision. The white van never stopped. He cruised past before I could exit my vehicle, preventing me from viewing his tag number.

Sanchez pulled in behind me some sixty seconds later. I pointed in the van's direction, and he took off in the same direction. While filling my gas tank, I listened to the officer's search for the van. No one saw it again. I was at a loss.

I called Sanchez and asked for a favor, "can you ride by my house and check it out? I'm returning to Jo's, just to make sure the van didn't double back on us." I nodded and hit the gas pedal, squealing my tires on the way out of the lot. There was no way I could sleep wondering if the white van returned to Jo's.

Jo and I spoke on the phone while I cruised the streets around her house. I found nothing but something niggled at me. Finally, giving in to exhaustion, I went home. Sanchez sat in my drive, never seeing the van. I thanked him for his troubles.

As I laid in bed, I was almost afraid to close my eyes for fear of an emergency. There is something I'm missing, but I don't know what. Finally, my eyes closed, and I slept until my alarm sounded. I texted Jo before my feet hit the floor. She was okay too.

Today might break the case wide open if we can get a message to Lyle. I prayed it worked because we had three days left in October, and with November looming, we expected another murder. But where and when was anyone's guess?

The team beat Westerly into the office, and when he showed, we followed him into the conference room. We wanted to be a part of his test. He spent time with his analyst friend this morning, getting advice on the best way to add the message. Our goal was to send it to Lyle and have it undetected by Erik.

While we watched Westerly, Conner called Jo. I cringed as she stepped out of the room. Westerly gave me a sideways glance because he knows how I feel about Jo. She returned and offered, "Conner called for a repeat date, but I declined. I told him we were close to capturing our killer." The niggle returned. Is Conner working with Erik?

Cabello called my cell with crime scene evidence from Jones' death. The fibers found in the car match the others from previous murders, and the killer used a 9 mm caliber handgun to murder Jones. I thanked him for the information, and then I relayed it to the group.

I paced the room while the thoughts sorted themselves out. If Erik doesn't own a gun, does Conner? "Did anyone ask for a weapons report on Conner?" Jo's mouth dropped.

"You don't think he killed Jones, do you?" Jo asked with her eyes wide, and eyebrows raised.

"I'm unsure who killed Jones. We need to tie up loose ends." I stated but something doesn't seem right here.

No one acknowledged Conner's weapon report, so I pulled it myself. Then I whistled as I returned to the office. "Conner is the proud owner of a 9 mm handgun. It's time for a surprise visit."

Jo, Sanchez and Schiller stood. I pointed to the computer and told Westerly to stay with it. We'd return for an update. I turned to leave and glanced over my shoulder to see Jo and the others following. We took two cars so we could enter Conner's business and have Sanchez and Schiller as back up in a neighboring lot.

It shocked Conner when we entered the building. He stood at the reception desk, and his mouth opened when he saw Jo, then his eyes turned dark when he looked at me. I asked him about the gun.

He glanced at Jo then back to me. "I keep it my vehicle for protection. Come on, I'll show you."

We followed him to his work van. He leaned inside and looked beside the console. "It's gone. Someone must have taken it." Then he showed Jo where he usually stored it, and as she leaned inside, she placed her hands on the floorboard for balance. But she came away from the truck with fibers pinched between two fingers.

She winked as she looked at me. I watched her take tissue from her bag, dab her eye, place the fibers in the tissue, then reach her hand into her jacket pocket. She did all she could to prevent cross-contamination, but hopefully, she plucked enough fibers for a comparison.

I looked at Conner and stated, "do not leave the area without our knowledge." He nodded as we left.

"His gun is conveniently missing, don't you think?" I questioned Jo.

"Yeah. He's bugging me. Is he withholding information, Ryker?"

"Time will tell." I radioed Sanchez of our return to the office, and they fell in behind us as we passed them.

We returned to the office, and Jo headed off to the lab to deposit her fibers. While we can't use the results in court, it will help in the investigation.

I returned to Westerly's side. "Bartley, I sent the message a few minutes ago, but I haven't received a reply."

As the clock struck noon, we moaned. No reply from Lyle. Now, we wait for Lyle's afternoon log-in time. During our wait, we revisited several crime scenes. Westerly spent time with the evidence, too, coming away with no new areas to focus on.

"Bartley, if you hadn't spotted the pattern with the dates of death, weekdays and street numbers, this guy could have conceivably operated for decades," Westerly emphasized.

"Someone would have caught on when he made a mistake. And we know they all make mistakes." I added.

Westerly called his analyst friend again, and we discussed options. After a debate, we agreed to wait until tomorrow to try again. If Erik stands over Lyle while the computer is active, Lyle can't take the chance to reply. We're already putting him in a predicament because he might have to hide the message from Erik.

When the analyst told us to back off, it made perfect sense. If Lyle could see the message in the code, so could Erik. We didn't want Lyle to die because of a message.

The afternoon seemed long. It always does when you're waiting on something. We stared at the computer for an hour. Then, when nothing happened, we left.

My night was quiet, but I had another run, and I felt better with myself as my mind relaxed. I cleaned the kitchen as I worked through the case. How has this guy kept Lyle alive for a week? He must be somewhere with food and water. But where? The same rolled around in my mind as I tried to sleep.

Midmorning of the following day, the lab called Jo with our results on Conner's truck fibers. The tech confirmed the fibers were from the same make of vehicle, just not Conner's. While happy to hear it, Jo still feels Conner is withholding information. Maybe she should meet him one more time.

Jo entered the room where Westerly and I worked on the computer. She reiterated the lab results. I pulled the motor vehicle report for Erik, and he and Conner drive the same make of work van. Is Erik setting up Conner for the fall? Why did that jump into my brain?

Today, Jo worked on Erik and Conner's social media while Westerly and I toyed with the CCTV footage. We had several areas we were concentrating on for the white van. My primary concern was the roads surrounding Jo's neighborhood. I spotted a white van passing the neighborhood before Jo's, but traffic prevented me from viewing the tag.

Westerly ran a check on Lyle's IP address again. He gasped. "Hey, Bartley. Can you step over here for a second?"

As I walked up, Westerly explained. "This is today's IP address check. Erik rerouted it again. Can you find the common area?"

I rolled a chair closer to the screen. "Give me a minute." As I studied it, the lines faded once I ruled them out. My mind works in odd ways sometimes. It's like it knows what I'm doing, and it helps by removing clutter. "There it is." I pointed to the same general area as before.

"Nothing changed. Thank goodness. When I saw the new configuration, I thought Erik moved Lyle." Westerly explained.

"He's still wherever he was before. My guess is Erik's house, but I have no way to prove it." I rolled myself back to my side of the table to continue my computer work.

A few minutes later, Jo asked to see us. We met at her desk. She explained her plan and asked us to back her up. So, we did. We sat there while she dialed Conner asking for an afternoon coffee break. He accepted.

Once the lunchtime crowd dispersed, Jo walked to the coffee shop two blocks from the office. She waited for Conner outside on the sidewalk. They ordered their drink choices and took a table in the front corner of the shop. Jo apologized to Conner for Ryker's behavior about the missing gun as she watched his eye twitch. Then Conner smiled as he stared at someone entering the café. Finally, Jo turned her head and watched Erik saunter over to their table.

Conner invited Erik to join them, and Jo grimaced but remained in her seat. Her coffee gave her hands something to do while trying to decide if she should run or stay.

The guys spoke for a few seconds like Jo wasn't there. Conner told Erik he and Jo had a coffee date and Erik's demeanor changed instantly. Then Erik dove into questions about the case while staring at Jo. She answered with bits and pieces of information, with the biggest topic being the gun. Conner's eye twitched as he stared at Erik.

Erik's facial expression never wavered. He should be a poker player because no one could read his face.

Jo sipped coffee as she studied the guy's converse. Finally, Erik left, citing work, leaving Conner and Jo sitting at the table. Jo tried to get Conner talking about Erik, but he refused. They left a few minutes later with Jo knowing Conner held the information she needed.

When Jo sat in her car, she plucked her phone from her jacket pocket and said, "Did you get that, Ryker?"

"Yeah, we got it. Did you know Erik was joining your coffee date?"

"Nope. Erik surprised Conner too. I wonder how Erik knew where to find him."
I paused and glanced at Westerly. "That's an excellent question. Is he following Conner or you?"

When Jo didn't reply, I said, "Come on back to the office. We're waiting for Lyle's reply." Jo clicked off without saying a word. She's consumed with the thought of Erik following her. Jo drove several side streets with her eye to the rearview mirror, and when she spotted a white van and called me.

Standing, I stated, "I'll meet you in the lot." I told Westerly and trotted out the door.

As Jo pulled into the lot, I stood beside my car. She exited her vehicle before stating, "the van turned off a block before the office. He stayed back so far I couldn't see the driver."

Once we made it to our room, I asked Jo for her take on the conversation with Erik and Conner. "Conner's eye twitches at the mention of the missing gun. I think he assumes Erik stole it, but I can't get him to talk to me about it."

Westerly whistled and motioned for us to join him. He shared Lyle replied to us when he logged into the computer. The reply was brief. Either he didn't have time to answer, or he was afraid it was a joke. Westerly sent another message asking his location.

Now, there was nothing to do but wait, so we left for home. I headed straight for the closet because I planned on running another night. As I reached for jogging clothes, I noticed the box. The box I had opened for Madge's clothes. Was I ready to handle this task?

After I stared at the open box for a few seconds, I shook my head, changed clothes, and trotted out the front door. I couldn't do it.

The evening temps were perfect for a run. I didn't bother with tunes because I needed to pay attention to my surroundings. While several vehicles entered the subdivision, the white van didn't.

I returned home and jumped into the shower. Then I stood over the box, taking a deep breath as I looked into the opening. Plucking a few garments from the hangers, I folded them before laying them in the box. The more I did, the easier it became, and within minutes, that job ended. I was proud of myself for finishing this step, knowing more lay ahead of me.

When I laid down, I dreamed of Madge. I saw her smiling face everywhere. While we had our issues, I missed her, and I would always love her.

At 11:00 am the next day, we sat huddled around Westerly's computer. We didn't have to wait long for Lyle's reply, which was a letdown. He doesn't know his location, only that it is a plain room with carpet. The rest of his message was cryptic. It was a row of numbers, but were they random? The numbers were 1108202111211108. Then it stopped. That's all he gave us. Westerly glanced at me.

I wrote them on a pad of paper, then I added. "I'll need to study these. Wonder why he stopped typing?"

Westerly raised his eyebrows before stating, "Erik may have interrupted him." Then he moaned.

I took the row of numbers to my desk and began studying their meaning. As a row, they meant nothing, but if I broke them apart, I might have something.

Erik plans a murder on 11/08/2021, with the street addresses being 1108 or 1121.

Gathering the team, I shared the latest development. We agreed we couldn't watch every house in the state with these addresses. Then I exclaimed, "the murder will be Dallas." Holding Jo's worksheet, I explained my idea. Greta nodded as I spoke. With the number of matching street addresses, we need another way. Since our plan didn't come to fruition, we left for lunch.

With the sun shining and a gentle breeze, we enjoyed lunch outside with a gaggle of other folks. We discussed the case and Lyle. Jo dropped her eyes to her drink, then back up. I waited because I felt a bombshell coming. She looked at me, "you know my street number is 1108." Then she dropped her eyes again.

That statement was a sucker punch to the gut because I'd paid no attention to her street number. I swallowed and then offered, "the killer has always chosen his murder victim with month and year. He has no reason to change it now."

"Unless the killer is Erik. He was angry that I met Conner for coffee. You should have seen his eyes." Jo shakes her head from side to side as she remembers the date.

I had no reply because anger bubbled inside me. "Why don't you stay with me until this thing blows over? I've got plenty of extra space."

"Ryker, I can't do that. We need to get this guy, and here's our chance. Is he planning two attacks on the same night?"

Jo's question triggered a notion. Would Erik change his process? We are closer to capturing him, and if he suspects it, he might try to make a statement. We finished lunch and returned to the office. I had several ideas to run past the others.

When we made it back, we were alone. Westerly had an errand to run, and Schiller and Sanchez passed us on the way inside. No one knew of Greta's status. I wanted to discuss my plan with Greta before I presented it to the group. Since she was away, Jo would have to lend an ear.

I studied Jo as she pecked away at her computer. Stress lines creased her eyes and forehead. She wouldn't admit it, but this scares her, and who could blame her. Serial killers are scary. "Jo, do you have a minute? I have a potential plan for Erik, but I want your opinion since we think this guy has his sights on you."

She laid her pen down and replied, "sure, go ahead." There wasn't much gusto in her reply, but I offered my idea. For Jo, we would have several detectives inside her house ready to apprehend Erik. Then Dallas would maintain roving patrols since the number of homes is monumental. There is no way to monitor each potential house unless we know which people turned Erik down for service.

Jo's head bobbed as I explained. "It sounds like our best plan is my place. I sure hope you're right on the meaning of those numbers."

I hoped I was right, too, because those numbers continue to roll around in my brain and no other combination makes sense, so I am sticking to it.

Since Jo agreed with the plan, I emailed and sent a text alerting the team to a 2:00 pm meeting, including the commanders, because I needed everyone on board. Then I spent an hour preparing for the meeting because I left nothing to chance. After all, Jo was the topic, and I couldn't live with myself if something happened to her.

At 1:45 pm, I entered the conference room. I logged into the computer and centered the camera for the table. Westerly joined us for the meeting. Others joined over the next several minutes as I prepared my speech.

Everyone joined today. I introduced Westerly to the team and thanked him for his help in front of the commanders. Then, with my notes in front of me, I shared Lyle's situation, his potential location and his replies to Westerly's messages. Then, I moved forward with my idea involving Jo.
Once I laid my idea on the table, slowly all heads nodded. I asked for questions or concerns then I waited.

Cabello spoke first, "Any idea how we can protect our Dallas residents?"

"That's why we're here. I'd like to see if we can come up with an idea other than roving patrols. If Erik is the killer, we stand a better chance of capturing him at Jo's than in Dallas, especially if his victim lives alone. It might be days before we hear of the murder." I paused, then I continued. "My best guess is Erik kills people who turned him down for a security system. Without his appointment calendar, we have no way to know who had an appointment with him or when. This is merely a guess. Two of our murder victims had appointments with ECE or EC listed in their calendars."

"Roving patrols is the only way. What about stopping white vans cruising around in the middle of the night?" Garcia offered.

Tiller joined the discussion by adding, "roving patrols are the only efficient way I see. No department has enough officers to sit on the number of possible residences nor the personnel to stop every white van."

The other three commanders agreed. Then Detective Morton asked, "Bartley, how did you determine Jo a target?"
First, I showed the group the number string that Lyle sent Westerly. Then when I broke the string down, I told the group Jo's street address is 1108. Finally, I asked her to describe her coffee date. She

did, and eyes grew wide, then they turned to slits as everyone realized the danger.

After Jo, I eased their pain with my plan. Westerly, Hutton, and I would hide inside Jo's place and prepare to take Erik down. Dallas would set its own roving patrol schedule. No one questioned the plan, especially since one of their own is a target.

Once the meeting ended, my thoughts moved to Lyle. We sat around the computer waiting for the clock to strike at 4:00 pm. Over the hour, no one spoke. Our eyes remained on the cursor, willing something to happen. We moaned when it didn't, and I leaned back in my chair and rubbed my neck.

Where is Lyle, and why didn't he reply? I sure hope Erik hasn't murdered him. He's just a kid.

I invited Jo to dinner, hoping it would calm her nerves. But as I sat across from her, I realized nothing would calm her until this ordeal was behind us. So, following Jo home, we kept an eye out for white vans. She pulled into her garage when we saw none, and I drove home thinking about tomorrow night.

Chapter 15

I woke to a partly sunny day after a somewhat decent sleep. When I stepped outside, the temps were warmer than yesterday, but a slight chill crossed your arms occasionally. The chill reminds us winter is on its way.

The office was quiet when I entered. As I sat alone, I studied the worksheet again then I moved to the number string. When I found no changes, I strolled to the coffee bar. Scenarios ran through my mind at a breakneck speed, and I wondered what I missed. If Lyle would reply to us this morning, we could scoop him up before tonight's activity. That would make for a perfect day.

When the group arrived, no one spoke much. Instead, they worked on different things, but at 11:00 am, we came together and stared at Westerly's computer cursor again. Again, no activity. Worry lines etched into Greta's forehead as she stated, "we haven't heard from him in over twenty-four hours." Heads bobbed as acknowledgment, but no one spoke.

Greta called a meeting after lunch because she wanted to revisit our plan. Officer Hutton and Westerly joined the meeting too. We discussed the plan again and decided on no changes. Our plan was in motion. While I was sorry Dallas had no way to find their victim, I was content knowing we would capture Erik tonight.

We left the office for home shortly after the meeting. Greta suggested a nap, but I couldn't calm my mind. Every time my eyes closed, the scene played out in front of me, and I couldn't wait to get my hands on that killer.

When darkness fell, Westerly, Hutton, and I entered Jo's through the back door. Sanchez and Schiller parked one road over from Jo's, so they could watch the front.

Officer Hutton moved upstairs while Westerly and I stationed ourselves downstairs. I opted to cover the back door because I wanted this guy with every fiber of my being. Jo tried persuading me to let Westerly have the back door, but I refused. She didn't want to see me get hurt, and I had no intention of letting him hurt me.

We wore ear comms so we could communicate with each other along with Greta and Tiller. In addition, the comms allowed for whispers so we wouldn't have to give away our location.

While trying to act normal, Jo cleaned her kitchen and folded laundry. She wanted to stare out the back windows waiting for Erik, but I encouraged her to change her focus. We didn't want to spook Erik, and we would if he caught her staring through one of the back windows.

At 10:00 pm, she went upstairs to bed. She read until 11:00 pm, then the lights went out. Since

Hutton was in her closet, she thought about talking with him, but then everyone would hear their conversation in the comms. So, she didn't. Instead, she stared at the ceiling, waiting for the attack.

At 2:45 am, our ear comms jumped to life. Greta told us Erik shot a man in Dallas. While Erik was inside the house, the man's girlfriend arrived in time to see Erik. Her presence scared Erik, and he ran as she touched the panic button on the alarm pad, but nothing happened. She dialed 911, and cops responded quickly since they were in the area. Erik escaped out the back. Greta emphasized our need to stay awake and prepare ourselves for an imminent attack.

Even though we sat ready, I wondered if Erik would attempt another murder tonight since the first one didn't go as planned. No one asked Greta if the Dallas man survived the gunshot.

At 3:15 am, I had my answer. Someone walked up the deck steps. I watched the shadow approach the door, then the doorknob moved. Taking a chance, I whispered to the group, letting them know Erik stood at the door.

Westerly shifted positions by entering the hall bath. This move placed him closer to me and to the action. We felt two against a serial killer was better than one.

The intruder entered without a peep. I let him cross the threshold and take three steps inside Jo's kitchen before I stood and yelled, "drop your weapon and raise your hands."

When Westerly flicked the lights on, the intruder froze. Westerly entered the room with his gun aimed at the guy's chest because there would be no missing the target with that distance. The guy wore all black with only the whites of his eyes visible. I think it's Erik, but until I had the mask removed, I wasn't 100% convinced.

The guy stood in place while considering his options. His eyes shifted between Westerly and me. Then he focused on me, and I prepared for the fight.

Our intruder lunged at me, and I stepped left, swinging upward with my right hand, which connected with his jaw. He staggered backward, rubbing his jaw. He has no idea of my background in hand-to-hand combat.

Westerly yelled again, and Hutton descended the stairs. When the intruder spotted Hutton walking toward the action, he tried me again, and this time I left him on the floor with a bloody nose.

Hutton and Westerly flipped him over and placed handcuffs on his wrists. Jo entered her kitchen, watching the action. She walked over to the guy and ripped the mask from his head.

That action confirmed Erik as our killer. He had the gun in his hip holster, which we would compare to the other murders. Next, we needed Lyle.

Erik seemed dazed, but I questioned him about Lyle. He refused to talk, but it didn't deter me. With him in custody, a judge would sign a warrant for his residence.

Sanchez and Schiller entered Jo's and took Erik to the office for us. He'd sit in a holding cell for a few hours, then I'd get to interrogate him. While I expected him to say nothing, I still wanted the opportunity.

Greta spoke through the ear comms that a judge signed a warrant for Erik's residence. She would notify us when she had it and for us to travel to Erik's. Just as we entered the neighborhood, Greta gave us the news that we had the warrant.

The group descended on Erik's house in the wee hours of the morning. The battering ram split Erik's door at the frame. We cleared Erik's first floor then we took the steps upstairs. Calling out for Lyle on our way up, we heard nothing. The owner's suite looked like any other. Then, as we walked across the catwalk to a bonus room, we heard a muffled cry.

Without a thought, I shouldered the door. Lyle sat in the middle of the room, bound and gagged. His shoulders relaxed when he recognized us. Jo removed the gag and hugged him while I worked to remove his bindings.

We notified Greta, and she instructed an ambulance is on the way. Lyle was quiet at first, but then he opened up about his ordeal. He described days sitting in the chair tied and gagged. The only movement was the computer two times a day until the end. He's been in the same position for over a week. We followed the ambulance to the hospital and congregated in the waiting room.

Once Lyle saw a doctor, they admitted him. While his vital signs appeared normal, they saw other signs of organ failure. With time, the doctors gave Lyle a good chance at a full recovery.

After we got word on Lyle's condition, I headed straight for the interview room. Erik was mine, but Westerly joined me. Erik continued his refusal to speak. He never wavered. It's as if he flipped a switch, and he now sits in a catatonic state. Neither Westerly nor I have seen anything like this.

Without Erik talking, we made a case without him. The bonus room was a treasure trove of evidence. We found the garotte laid on a plastic table along with multiple ammo boxes. The table was where Erik planned his murders because he marked his past murders on a map. This sealed the deal.

Jo found a folder full of old job applications dating back several years where Erik applied for a position as a police officer with multiple departments. Each application had a denial letter attached. That fits right in with our profile.

Several days later, the crime lab techs confirmed Erik's gun actually belonged to Conner. We surmise he stole it from Conner because we found no connection between the murders and Conner. He also provided critical details to Erik's killing spree. Erik married in July, and they divorced in November. That answered our questions about Erik's murders occurring only in July and November.

The most satisfying step in this process is to witness a serial killer sentenced to prison for life without a chance at parole. The team exited the courthouse with smiles on our faces for a job well done. But then I wondered if Erik kept a book with his future plans in it. If he does, I can only hope no one finds it.

ABOUT THE AUTHOR

A.M. Holloway is an author of murder, mystery, crime, thriller, and suspense books with a little romance for added excitement. She was born and raised in Georgia and still lives in the northwest part of the state. When not writing, you will find her with family enjoying the outdoors or sitting in her favorite chair daydreaming about her next book.

Other Books by A.M. Holloway

Murder for Justice (Digger Collins Thriller Book 2)

Flames of Murder (Mac Morris Thriller Book 2)

Promises of Murder (Sheriff Jada Steele Book 1)

Pieces of Murder (Digger Collins Thriller Book 1)

MOA (Mac Morris Thriller Book 1)

~~~~~~~~~~~~~~~

Visit **www.amholloway.com** for new releases and to sign up for my reader's list or simply scan the code.

70333763R00173